CANNIBALS

Dan Collins lives in West Cork, Ireland.

Dan Collins

CANNIBALS

V

VINTAGE

Published by Vintage 2002

1 3 5 7 9 10 8 6 4 2

Copyright © Dan Collins 2001

Dan Collins has asserted his right under the Copyright,
Designs and Patents Act, 1988 to be identified as the author
of this work

First published in Great Britain by
Jonathan Cape 2001

Vintage
Random House, 20 Vauxhall Bridge Road,
London SW1V 2SA

Random House Australia (Pty) Limited
20 Alfred Street, Milsons Point, Sydney,
New South Wales 2061, Australia

Random House New Zealand Limited
18 Poland Road, Glenfield,
Auckland 10, New Zealand

Random House (Pty) Limited
Endulini, 5A Jubilee Road, Parktown 2193,
South Africa

The Random House Group Limited Reg. No. 954009
www.randomhouse.co.uk

A CIP catalogue record for this book
is available from the British Library

ISBN 0 09 928668 8

The Random House Group Limited supports The Forest Stewardship
Council® (FSC®), the leading international forest-certification organisation.
Our books carrying the FSC label are printed on FSC®-certified paper.
FSC is the only forest-certification scheme supported by the leading
environmental organisations, including Greenpeace. Our
paper procurement policy can be found at
www.randomhouse.co.uk/environment

MIX
Paper | Supporting
responsible forestry
FSC
www.fsc.org
FSC® C018179

Printed and bound in Great Britain by Clays Ltd, St Ives plc

to my family

contents

cannibals

A Thing About Hotels

. . . Nick has a thing about hotels. They excite him. Ask him to explain and he mumbles on about the anonymity, the security, the ideally sterile, functional nature of the rooms, the impersonal decor, the erasability of all trace of one's passage through the space, the absolution of clean sheets sullied by whatever urge takes you or accident befalls you, housekeeping will see that you leave without remark . . . I sometimes upset him by talking about the filthy habits of hotel guests. The scant regard for hygiene. The peeing and worse in the sinks. The wank on the sheets. The snot on the headboard. The blood on the towels. And you're not even safe in an extortionately priced, snooty establishment in the West End or Knightsbridge. What better to soil than a Philippe Starck spanking modern decor. That's what I think. There are always strange, sick people out there doing the unimaginable. You learn not to be surprised.

Adultery

One other thing I'm discovering about this period of my life is the mostly insignificant fact that proportionately more of the men I'm attracted to are married than at any time previously. And if like me you're not obsessed by matrimony, couldn't care less about it, the institution or the fading prospect, in fact abhor it for the, well, for lots of reasons, one of which is not, I might add, the hitherto lack of proposals directed at me personally, no, I'm not bitter about that, then it's no drawback to carrying on like I am, in fact it's an absolute boon. And on the very rare occasions when the lack of unattached men begins to weigh, then there's always adultery. Believe me, it's no skin off my nose.

Advice

Get an education they said. I got one. Get a job they said. I got one. Get a man they said. I got one. Then I got a dozen. Then a hundred. Get saved they said. Get away they said. Get help they said. It wasn't so much that I stopped listening. More like I'd never been listening. Ever. Not even when I was doing what they were telling me to do. It just sort of happened there was a coinciding between what they were telling me to do and what I was doing anyway before they stuck their noses in my business and spewed all their mustered fucking shite out of their big, useless gobs.

Amanda

On the streets or in bed or up the mountain or out in the desert off on weekends it goes on, remains essentially the same, captured alive, twisting, exposed, displayed, an endless series of unpleasant days and nights. I'm told the outcome is in my hands but I know I'm not a participant-slash-contestant in this fegary, never was, never aimed to be. Frankly my little spells do nothing to improve my situation. I should know by now. A crow should know. A dog should know. A stone should know. A single heartbeat, I shall die dead, falling over backwards, yesterday, today, tomorrow, tripping over myself. First things first I was told, but that's a disgustingly outmoded concept if you want my pennyworth. Man and woman. Frank does Gloria, Gloria does Jerry, Jerry does Myra who remembers doing Frank not all that long ago. Half-truths, innocent play, some sense of what could arise. I've marvelled at those of my acquaintance, Frank, Gloria, Jerry, Myra, who have that capacity. Marvelled. They tell me I'm known for my malice. Specifics, I say. Give me specifics. The time I led X to believe Y was telling the world and its mother all about certain scarcely moral dealings in what we termed Mexican fertiliser. I find it difficult to breathe in the face of such crap. Some people are just so dangerous, they ought never be invited in, they ought never be confided in, they twist everything. I'm too thin, I'm too fat, I'm not eating the right foods, I'm not exercising enough, I'm exercising too much, I'm too private, I'm too smart, too dumb, too selfish, too aloof, too tan, too pale, too blond, too gray, too late, too early, too this, too that, too yah, too yea. I live on dead-end Montana Street with my back to Elysian Park, my nose to downtown. The neighborhood is going to shit. The city has tagged too many quake-damaged properties no one cares enough to bulldoze or renovate. More and more the gangsters come to stand on the corner of Douglas and Montana. They know I call the cops to complain about them. I've guns enough and grilles and leave my paper targets from the range pinned around the place, headshots proving my prowess at close quarters. I see my children when they are in town. They stay with their father, naturally. His house is more commodious. It has power and so forth. I have my own comforts. I keep my mind agile through means of algebra and baseball scores. I count pores, my pores, thronging with pores I am. I am trying to have all of it, keep all of it balanced so finely, so finitely, in my mind. I understand acutely what must occur should I lose my sense of that balance. It is a wearying and, at times, cruel taskmistress. I dare not blink . . . by times . . .

this, this service redeems me. I am particular about the milk I'm brought. Thank you, Mrs Rodriguez. I keep a herb garden on the roof. I have in the forenoon been known to skip rope, my shoes slapping up the fine dust of the yard, listening to Radio Korea coming from the open windows of the bungalows below me, old women hunched over sewing machines, humming. Walking in the park I step around ritual traces, scattered candies, half-smoked cigars, broken branches, smashed crockery, empty rum bottles, magic worked by small, round, dark, long-skirted women I know to see. All the neighborhood cats are gone, vanished, presumed dead, sacrificial tokens. I try not to brood. Everything must be kept smooth and lucid, not a hint of a smudge on the slick plane. My good side is my left. When the authorities come to visit I show them my left. When the media and the historians and the ghouls strive to pick over me and my freakish surviving bones, my once famous bones, I bow my head and feign grouchy devotion, shunting beads and mumbling contritely. That usually throws them. If not, I take to my heels, in my own way venerating flight, interceding with no greater entity than escape. It was a circus, is all I'll say about the old days, a horror show, not eating only shrinking, wasting, one day after another. Now it seems a cheap trick we played on the world but then I'm still around to complain, old misery guts, steaming out in the open, embarrassing everyone. I don't want to talk about it. I'll never understand another thing. I've promised myself I shall die dead falling over backwards one of these tormented days out in the open, the street, the roof, the park, the mountain. Backwards, so I shall gaze lastly at the endless sky. Any moment now, any moment.

Another Thing About Hotels

My friend, who professes to be too busy to get married, comes to town on business and calls me up, suggesting we meet at his hotel. The hotel he's staying in is on the Strand. And as I've never been here before I'm conscious of appearing a little lost as I step into the foyer and search for the elevator and the most direct route to his room. I always feel nervous in hotel foyers. Even under the most innocuous of circumstances I feel as though I'm flying a gaudy banner drawing attention to myself, identifying me as one of those unfortunate women in the movies who are invariably accosted by hotel management and accused of being up to no good as a brutal prelude to being shown the door and shunted back onto the street where they belong. Of course, it doesn't help on this occasion that I know that I'm up to no good. But I'd like to see anyone lay a hand on me and suggest such a thing. It wouldn't be a pretty sight. Of course, as it transpires, no one pays me the least notice and my heart is beating a little fast as I shoot up in the elevator, pleasantly cocooned. I'm scheming how annoyed I'm going to let on to be with him for failing to offer to meet me in the lobby or the bar or even outside on the street. But when I step into his room we hit it off right away and I'm glad he called and suggested we get together.

The room is plush and we make ourselves at home, settling into the surroundings, becoming plush as plush can be. It's not long before he mentions again how his life is so hectic he hasn't the time to get married. And this time I never mentioned marriage, never brought it up, never said a word. I don't smile, don't react, nothing, don't rush in the bathroom to weep, don't get dressed and go home, do nothing like I may have done on other occasions we've been together, no, I just lie here in his bed and let it all float on by like it's a big old fluffy dream and nothing much to do with me. And this worries him, I know, my dispassion, my failure to react, because next morning he suggests somewhat sheepishly that perhaps we ought to get married after all and although I ache to say yes, I feel if I am to be consistent with my new ploy I really have no other option but to say why don't we take some time to think it over.

We're meeting for lunch and I'm wondering if that's time enough for me to gracefully condescend to accept his proposal. Though the more I think about it the more it seems that it was less of a proposal and more of a casual suggestion. Perhaps he thinks he's off the hook where I'm concerned by having issued such a fuzzy up-in-the-air gambit. Perhaps by lunchtime he'll have recovered his true nature and conveniently forgotten all about marrying me, put that option away once and for ever. Perhaps that's for the best. It would certainly be less fraught, less problematic, than always having to speculate about his true intentions.

Of course if that's how it's to be I shan't see him ever again . . . he'll come to town one day, give me a call, expecting me to drop everything, and then he'll find this particular boat has sailed, is no longer hiring out for pleasure trips. We shall have to wait and see though, shan't we.

Aoife

The one place you don't want to fly into if there's any weather is Kennedy. Aoife told this to me as we walked down Grafton Street. It was a choice between Bewley's or McDonald's. She said, You don't know what I'm like, Dan. Yes I do, I said. Aoife was thin-skinned and worked in television. She liked to switch subjects. One minute it would be something about Dennis Quaid and Meg Ryan, the next it would be her 'proud to be an omnivore' speech. In her company I could only think along the lines of her pale skin, dark crotch, and a song I'd heard somewhere, 'Slippery When Wet'. Then, as if

I was interested, she started telling me for what seemed like the thousandth time how she first met her boyfriend, Jerome, and how exquisitely soft his skin was. I said let's go for a drink but she wanted to go home so we hailed a taxi. She was ceaselessly voluble, ever chaste away from Jerome, had never seen a dead body, and was always anxious to keep in touch. Aoife sort of rubbed off on you. Jerome was often busy in London or Paris and I made a point of staying close to Aoife. We went to the same parties and she would confide in me, whispering warmly in my ear the pitiful none-too-evident defects of the other women present. I was on her side. I granted her credulity. I exaggerated the flaws she so imaginatively discerned. She talked of moving to London to be closer to Jerome. I tried to dissuade her. She asked me how many feminists does it take to screw in a light bulb? Two. One to screw in the bulb and one to suck your dick. Not my dick, she laughed. I said, Seriously, Aoife. Then she confessed she'd kept something from me. Jerome was married. Not to her, no, to another woman. They had a child but they weren't living together. And still she wanted to move to London. She asked me what I thought. I told her I didn't know what to say. I told her I didn't know what she wanted me to say. She shrugged and pouted and after a while I got up the courage to tell her she was crazy, that someone like Jerome would always let her down. She told me to leave and when I didn't she slapped me and I caught her and pinned her arms to her side and bundled her backwards so we stumbled onto the sofa. We struggled as I tried to kiss her. Her head crashed around. I kissed her. She lay still. She didn't move. She said nothing. And I knew I could do nothing more. I stood up and looked down at her where she lay half-on, half-off the sofa, breathing hard and quick, her eyes shut, her hair ruffled, her shirt untucked from her trousers. I mumbled an apology and went to the door. I turned to look back at her. Aoife, I said softly. But she didn't answer me. There were leaves on the street, yellow and brown leaves which crinkled underfoot, drifts of fallen leaves. I thought about Aoife. I thought about myself. I thought how one of us needed to get a grip on things. I thought how if I didn't get clear of Aoife I'd have to turn to basket-making. When I got home there was a message on my machine from Jerome. He needed to talk to me urgently. I called him up, hunched over the phone, a sense of doom thumping between my ears.

Arnica

Arnica, also known as leopard's bane. A traditional herbal cream for the symptomatic relief of bruises, wounds and swellings. Alma sends one of her juniors round with a tube of the stuff. Also an eye balm which reduces puffiness. Alma's girl stands astride her bicycle, scrutinising my face, trying to see beyond the dark glasses. She wears pressed, new, sand-coloured cargo pants, red runners without socks, a red scoopneck sweater. Her glossy coppery hair has come loose from a series of silver clips. Full breasts. Big white teeth. A scrubbed defiant face. She's seventeen.

Before We Were Married

I remember crying, 'Give way,' and champing on her ear, my beating stalled and vanishing, a distant puzzle inside of her. She shoved me off and I rolled onto my back, gasping, sweaty, veins throbbing on my neck and forehead. She sat up, turned her back on me and fingered her ear. She moaned and stepped out of bed and hurried to check in the mirror and promptly declared, 'You fuck, you bit my fucking ear off, you mauled me, I'm ruined, I'll need surgery, surgery won't do, you balls, oh, fucking hell!' And once that was out, she fell to the floor in a perfect heap, apparently completely dead. I didn't hurry to her side because I thought she was play-acting. Instead I stared at her paleness, her tiny breasts, her thin arms, her sharp-wrapped hip bones, the dark neat wedge of her sex, her smart jaunty nose, every bit of her nice work. When eventually I did arrive, I toed her gently in the small of her back and said, 'Come on now, come on.' And then I saw the blood steal in a slender line from beneath her hair and slowly move across her face towards her barely parted lips. I caught her under the arms and dragged her to the bathroom, and light as she was, her heels laid tracks through the carpet pile. I found her blood on my hands, my belly, my privates. I panicked. My heart flipped and I couldn't breathe. I splashed cold water on her face and dabbed at where I'd bitten her, and cried, 'Oh God, Oh God,' until she blinked and focused unhappily on me. 'You fucking bollocks butcher you,' she said, not at all gently, and fought a way out of my encircling arms. I was so happy and relieved that she was all right. I was grinning at her as she inspected the washed-out, now scarcely visible scratch on her ear, towelled her face, tidied her hair. 'Stop it,' she said, 'you look like an absolute moron.' 'I love you,' I said. 'That's too bad,' she said. 'You're too thin,' I said. 'Really?' she said. 'Oh, yes,' I said. 'You're not,' she said, 'just saying that to get in my good books?' 'No,' I said. And after a brief moment she said, 'Fuck you,' and started to cry and said again, 'fuck you.' Mystified and all as I was, that was the moment when I realised I had a chance with her. I took her in my arms, kissed and lapped at her tears, inwardly started to plan ahead, outline the life we'd have together . . . everything falling into place, nice house, holidays, a couple of kids, an OK combined income, blow jobs for Christmas. I wasn't sure how I'd gotten to that stage of wanting those things, that future, this particular woman, but I felt like I was a pioneer, you know, breaking a new trail, going where no man had been before. And all the time I never suspected she was there, always one step ahead of me, leading me on.

Being Stalked

Have I ever been stalked? Yes, I've been stalked. Several times in fact. Only this last year, 4 August to 17 August, I was stalked by an unwashed red Volkswagen *Passat* with a hitch on the back . . . the ball type of hitch which an unsuspecting pedestrian passing between parked cars might walk into and crack their shins on. Which is how I first came to notice the pervert inside.

Betty

Business is slipping. Business is lousy. Before I point this out to her I need to consider what her response might be, how she might defend herself whatever I say, because if I don't know what she's like no one does. Eileen Mulvagh is her name and there are elements of born overachiever to her. You know the type, decked ever in linen and lipstick. I don't know that she's lied or schemed or screwed to get to where she is. I honestly don't know. Years ago I remember her as charming, amiable, a softness encompassing her. Now she is strident and harassing. I think it has to do with the pressure of business, the souring of prospects, but still she has the air of one to whom the cause of improvements is paramount, her mainstay. That's the line she gives off anyhow. Seven years ago she had a son with a local celebrity many years older than her, a politician, a builder, a married man to tell the truth, and somehow she never let the fact of her being a single parent interfere with her reputation. Not that I believe she should have gone around volunteering remorse or contritely grinding out her youth or anything. It's her business. But when she brings the boy to me to look after then I have to start feeling entitled to some say in her life. It's not that I want to tell her what to do. It's just I don't see that I should dangle here while she waltzes pretty around town. Any time I try to raise the issue she kind of shrugs and makes this face which I take to mean where do I think she gets it from. I let on there isn't an answer to that kind of notion even though I know she considers me an old hippie and likely to relate to all types of lax thinking. My man friend tells me I'm being a menopausal bore. This kind of abuse I've come to expect from him as a prelude to fairly satisfactory sex, so why should I object to his siding with her. Initially I used to worry about Eileen's bleak and mute disapproval of my acquiring a man friend so late in the day but lately he and Eileen have established some mysterious truce. When the boy comes to stay with me, and my man friend takes him off to the river or the driving range, I know he's coaching him in musty man things and relishing the role. I honestly can't see why I'm making so much out of this. I like my life. I like the way it's worked out. But there's something niggling, some incipient cloud which, when it finally storms over me, I'm going to be able to say I knew it, I knew it all along, and everyone will have to salute my perspicacity, hormonal deficiencies and all.

Bianca

No one talks about my past. My ordeal. No one asks any questions. I don't ask. They don't ask. I don't volunteer any details. They send me to school. School is a movie. These girls they have there are in a glamour mania. Tall. Thin. Clean. Pale. I move among them like I'm one of them. But I'm not. I know I'm not. I'm dead. I'm waiting to be discovered and dug up and displayed and paraded around like a bleeding relic.

Billy

Then one day Billy turns up at the Mundys' house in Los Feliz. He's there at the end of the driveway. Looking right at me. And then he smiles and I run and leap into his arms and he turns me round and round until we're both dizzy and he stumbles away, bearing me like this until we collapse in a pile on the lawn. A soft landing with the sprinklers swishing hazily over us. He wants me to go away with him. I'm going nowhere. He's not listening. I want to know where he's been. He only wants to talk about what's to come. I touch his cheekbones. He's so thin and gaunt. I wonder if he's been ill. He touches me. He touches my hand, my wrist, my forearm, my elbow, his fingers sliding slowly up into my armpit.

'Billy,' I say, leaning away from him.

Then I don't see him again for months.

Bloodsports

Henry Porter wants to drink my blood. The Henry Porter. Wee maybe but I say no to bloodsports.

Monday a.m. I fly Concorde to New York. Tuesday am in White Sands, New Mexico, being photographed by Adolfo Luna for *Vanity Fair*. Wednesday all day, meetings with agents in L.A. who seem disappointed as soon as I open my mouth. Like they've surely heard me speak before? Not that I ever gave a damn for movies. I could play myself they suggest half-heartedly. I tell them my time is valuable and walk. Thursday, date with a baseball player on pushy Sandy Eberhartz Mason's say-so, a teammate of her husband Tommy's. Big hands, small dick, so he fingers me and eats me out. He wants to marry me. I smile and say my goodbyes. He won't call. Even though it's me, Regina, the Regina. Friday, New York. The Royalton. Then Saturday, Concorde to Paris.

In my dreams Henry Porter quaffs my blood. Reception holds my calls. In the morning I find Henry Porter's left a stack of messages. Other callers too numerous to list. I wait for my period. I get my period. I go downstairs and get a mud wrap. Later, courier jiffy bag to Henry Porter with used Lil-let enclosed. At least someone's going to be happy today.

Bond Street

Everything has taken a tangible toll. Not a day goes by that I don't find another wrinkle, another fold in my skin, whipping up disorientating feelings of panic and loss. It's not that I have more idle time than others in which to dwell upon what are, after all, universal changes. It's me being me, half-believing there's been a dreadful mistake. God intended me to be the twenty-two-year-old clueless rustic virgin in a just-bought scarlet mohair puff-sleeved sweater I once was – yes, He did, He does, just ask Him – loping without a care along Bond Street on my way to meet Armand and pick up my engagement gift, a South Sea pearl necklace with diamond clasp which I now keep buried uninsured in a Hermès scarf in my knicker drawer. Would I ever want to stop being me and switch places with my daughter? Of course, provided I could keep the jewellery. I as Alice would want the baubles – to hock if not to wear the dated pieces.

Breaking Up

And Patrick's just yapping away, 'No rhyme nor reason to anything you say or do, nothing makes sense where you're involved.'

'Me? What about you? You're so infuriating. Oh! I don't know why I bother.'

And now we're walking out of the park, moving south along Regent's Park Road, traffic mewling by, indifferent to the two of us as we press on, going through the motions, prodding the dead thing that lies between us.

'You don't love me,' he says.

'Who said that?'

'You never said.'

'What? I never said what?'

'*I love you.*'

'I love you too,' I say, not sure why I'm saying it, not believing it for one moment.

'No?' he says, sounding surprised. 'I . . .' And looking strangely, wrong-footed, at me. 'You do?'

'What is it now, for God's sake? Why are you looking at me like that? What?'

And I get this idea that maybe I've made him happy for at least one second in our time together. And that makes me happy for just about the same fleeting measure of time.

And after that, who ever knows what comes next.

Because now I'm feeling this is quite an achievement for me and there's no more to be gained by hanging around. I'm going to be twenty-three in four months' time. I'm sleeping soundly again, experiencing little or no anxiety about still being single or resembling my mother physically or behaviourally. There's so much I haven't done. I'll tell him right away. Love doesn't last for ever. Sometimes love doesn't even last five minutes. Sometimes even less time passes before love changes into something else, something different, something less, a squabble for instance. And we're so lucky, honestly, to have had so much together, to have crammed so much into the time we've known each other. I feel I'm making progress. I've been mature enough to acknowledge love, mature enough to recognise when it's time for change. I'm sure Patrick will appreciate that I need to keep moving. The shark in me obliges me to swim, always swim. Furthermore, my lifeline is abnormally short – people have told me so, expert palm readers – and there's a lot of people I haven't met, a lot of places I haven't been. As for my immediate plans, if it's not going to be Bruce again, then maybe I'll go to Tokyo for a week and shop for shoes. I've never had an Oriental lover. I hear they're squat and chauvinistic and smell of fish and Cerruti aftershave.

'Patrick,' I say.

'Yes,' he says, looking worried.

I brace myself, telling myself I must be cruel to be kind. I say, 'I think I've made a terrible mistake.'

He takes one long last look at me and understands what I'm about to do and he tells me, 'So have I,' and he just turns and walks away.

Part of me is relieved and part of me sad and part of me just plain numb as I turn and shuffle towards home. I hope he doesn't feel I've been wasting his time. Years from now, occasionally, just before I fall asleep, I'll think of him, and confuse him with someone else, mix up parts of one with elements of the other, physical, character-wise, names, faces, sexual adroitness, locations we visited, parties we fled prematurely because we couldn't keep our hands off one another. Or maybe we'll run into each other in Paul Smith, him with his new girl, me with my Japanese lover, and we'll nod, and scantly acknowledge one another to avoid prolonged explications to our new companions of our lost significance to one another. It is this vague possibility which holds the most interest for me where Patrick is concerned. We were lovers, we almost married, he worked for a bank, I used to write lifestyle for the supplements, I went to Tokyo and found something different. That's all.

Naturally I don't even get to call Trailfinders and make a booking, never mind get to actually fly out to Tokyo. Four minutes after leaving Patrick, while cutting across Fitzroy Road, north towards Chalcot Square, this tan, balding, grey-stubbled guy in a spanking green Alfa Spider slows to ask me, 'Aren't you the bird from the television?'

He's not at all what I pictured a late-night viewer of Channel Four to be like, not at all the type to watch the kind of programme that would have me as a fleeting guest, the kind of programme where the presenter is barefoot and the audience clamours for her to get her puppies out for the boys. His name is Clive and even though he's married with two kids . . . the Spider's his wife's, by the way . . . and hasn't a notion of getting serious on me and leaving his wife or introducing me to his parents, friends or colleagues, we're off to Deauville for the weekend.

And if Patrick calls in the meantime?

He won't. I mean, why should he. I'm impossible.
I'm a serial maniser. I'm virtually debauched.

But if he calls?

I'm me. I'm not desperate, or needy. I'm whole,
I'm not in bits. And my instant success with Clive has
reassured me, if I needed reassuring, that I've lost none
of my appeal, none of my ability to bring men to their
knees.

But if he calls?

He won't.

But?

Why should he?

He loves me, I love him.

What's that mean in this day and age? Love? It's
such twaddle. It's old hat. It's not viable. It's not
healthy. It's restrictive.

Don't fool yourself, girl.

Then maybe I should call him?

Call him.

I'm still going to Deauville.

Call him.

I may do.

Call him now.

I will.

'Hello?'

'Yes?'

'Bruce, it's me, Georgie.'

'Georgie.'

'Have you missed me?'

'Oh, baby,' he says.

Broken Heart

'You broke my heart,' he said, blinking, his eyes smarting, brimming over. 'That's impossible,' I said. 'You goaded me,' he said, 'and then you broke my fucking heart.' 'You'll get over it,' I said. 'I won't,' he said, starting to whimper. I mean, please, who hit whom. I felt my cheek, realised something was blooming there, a deep abrasion, I was suddenly desperate to get to a mirror, fearing the skin was broken. Then I noticed his excitement, the lurid business end of his peeder bobbing away to itself down there. All I could think then was what a dubious accomplishment to get it so stirred up in present circumstances. I touched it gently, mindful of calamari, ink staining my lips, that briny flavour. Leading it all the way into my mouth. Ages of indifferent desultory sucking until he pushed me away, despairing of my ever bringing him off. With a hand on my shoulder for balance, he jerked himself desperately until he came on my face. 'I hope you're feeling better,' I said, 'I hope you're feeling very happy with yourself.'

Bunny's

Meanwhile, it seemed like a good way out, the barman started bringing us our drinks, we didn't even have to catch his eye, they'd just appear before us, a succession of pints, someone was paying or would pay later, I didn't know which, my grandmother had just died, she was ninety-three, and I'd been shortlisted for a literary prize which in itself didn't excite me as I'd been shortlisted before, many times in fact, nothing was cheering me up, not my new pal Dermot who insisted I call him Hector as he did a good business dealing speed to local Leaving Certs, convent girls by preference, not the prospect of Roisin driving down from Dublin with her family at the weekend, not the money I'd get once my grandmother's estate was probated or whatever they do in this shit-caked country, I was born in Chicago twenty-seven years ago with what I guess you'd have to call a silver spoon in my gob and all I could say about the intervening years was that I'd fucked up seriously somewhere along the line, I got to my feet and motioned to Hector that I was going for a slash, I must have been waiting for his permission because he waved me away and lifted his pint to his face and held it there until it was half-gone, as if it was all arranged I ran into the girl with the nose stud on the way to the bog, I leaned close and saw it was made of paste and she smiled and said she was running late but I should call her and I nodded, took it all in my ungrateful stride, more booty, she seemed concerned for me, apparently we were old acquaintances, and got up on tiptoes to kiss me on the cheek, I nodded and told her she was an angel of mercy and I swear to God, tears started up out of her eyes and she hurried away, I spent a good few minutes in the bog searching for my flies and another few minutes looking for my willie, it was like Siberia in there, you should have seen the steam off the piss, where was I, somewhere mundane, I started to list my requirements for the coming week, I needed sleep, I needed cash, I needed to retrieve my manuscript from Marina, I needed Roisin to sit on the edge of my bed and read what I'd written, I needed her to wear that sleazy low-cut backstreet dress she'd found in Liège, I looked down and saw where piss had run down the leg of my pants and pooled on my shoe, it was funny, and you had to be there, I stood under the hot-air drier for a couple of turns, guys had been coming and going all the time and one of them may have been Hector, I didn't engage, I was busy, someone told me a joke, how do you know when your sister's got her period, your father's dick tastes strange, I have no trouble remembering dumb jokes, when I got back to the table Hector was talking to three kids, two guys who had a girl in tow, I stood alongside the girl, I caught her wrist and brought her glass to my lips, she was drinking Pepsi Cola, I told her who I was, I told her I was born in Chicago, I told her she should go and live in Barcelona as soon as she finished school, I told her I wasn't desperate, I told her she had nice eyes, a trusting face and thrusting boobs, I was making her smile, the guys talking with Hector were starting to pay attention to me, I caught her wrist again and shucked an ice cube from her glass and crunched it loudly, I was growing bolder, more daring, I told her I was scandalised by the youth of today and without expecting an answer, asked her how old she was, I don't know if she answered, her eyes looked older than the rest of her which I know is a cliché but in her case true and she was a honey all right, I told her I was a perfect example of my type and waited for her to enquire further, but all I got was some whispered advice in my ear that I should shove off, I shrugged my shoulders, stared trash, mentioned Montaigne and faintly then Plutarch's *Lives*, I told her she was perfectly peachy and wondered whether she shaved underarm and if she didn't, whether it was damp matted black the way I preferred, she raised a hand, and I shied, but it was only to shove back unruly hair from her face and I gazed transfixed down along the loose open sleeve of her lemony Brazil football shirt to the satiny white bind of her brassiere's flank and the fuzzy tendrils of deodorised dry hair nestled there, it was tawny, faded brown, nothing to thrill a jaded eye, and then Hector was on his feet, an arm around me, an arm around princess, and the two dour boys glaring at us as we were steered towards the door, I abruptly felt anxious to acquire a new goal in life, we were going outside where the night sky was clear and star-ridden, the two boys, attendant gurriers, thugs, philistines, I was a shortlisted writer after all, it was cold outside, and when the beating came I half-regarded it as simulated, Hector and the girl watched and kissed all the while, I was impressed by their effortless perform-ance, snogging away while the two boys beat the shit out of me, she seemed boneless in his arms, relying on him to keep her from falling, giving herself to him, then the boys began telling jokes, I tried to tell the one I'd heard about the sister's monthly, my sister, their sister, Hector's sister, maybe that's who she was, it didn't matter whose sister she was but I couldn't get the words out, they were kicking me in the ribs and my mouth was full of blood

Callers

I know Holly must be dead or working at the BBC or married to someone like Keith from the Prodigy or Neil Back or even Stan Collymore or Michael Douglas, not that they're at all of a type, or at the very least she's discovered me in some unforgivably sordid predicament. I dropped in to see her friend Mary in Padstow before Christmas. She's left her husband and moved to Wadebridge with her two kids. She hinted at some dark doings on his part. I can't picture what he might have done that was so bad she had to leave him. He's such a quiet sad bastard. Though, now I think about it, maybe it was a mercy to leave him in peace. Anyway, I hope Holly's well and thriving wherever she is. I know I could track her down, call her. But she could call me just as easily. Couldn't she?

Calories

I'm not a junky, you know. I'm just a casual user, totally recreational. The first time I used, my friend Monique, Monique Singleton, now she's a junky, she asked me where I wanted it, like I was so naive, I never even imagined there was a choice, but when I thought about it, I knew I didn't want any holes in me where people could see, so that ruled out my arms, my neck, my legs. See this scarf, it's a Tom Ford, Gucci, it's like silk and ethnic, I got it from my boyfriend. He's a very important man. He loves me. When I suck his cock he fills me full of love. And you know that it's fattening, it is, it has so much, like a quadzillion calories in like just a tablespoonful, not that there's ever that much of the stuff. He's not that big on spunk. No. So this, I do this because, exactly because, like, an occasional hit of smack helps me keep my figure. And since my boyfriend never goes down on me, he doesn't notice the holes. So everything's cool.

Cannibals

'There, yes, lower, yes, that's it, that's the spot, right smack on the fucking nail, oh, yes, keep doing it to me, oh, harder, yes.'

'David.'

'What?'

'I don't think I should be doing this.'

'Why the fuck not?'

'It's not really in my job description.'

'Lorraine.'

'Yes.'

'You're not afraid of me, are you?'

'No.'

'You're not afraid of my wife?'

'No.'

'That's right, because my wife and I have an understanding. We don't talk, we don't live in the same house, we don't anything any more, you know.'

'I know.'

'Is it Jenny Lu?'

'She makes me feel . . .'

'She makes you feel what?'

'Small.'

'She's just my companion. A face for the nation to salivate over. A decoration for my arm at state functions, fancy-dan occasions. Jenny Lu is PR. Jenny Lu buys my suits and that's as far as it goes.'

'Are you sure, because I don't think that's what she thinks, the way she acts, draping herself all over you, it's practically obscene.'

'OK, maybe she is a little demonstrative.'

'Demonstrative?'

'It's all part of the package, don't you see, the illusion. Jenny Lu is candyfloss to reassure the public no matter that I live apart from my wife I remain as manly as ever. She is a bit of fluff to show I'm a healthy heterosexual with healthy heterosexual tendencies. That's Jenny Lu's purpose, her function, her business. That's what she's good at. But always remember, she's not my wife and she's not from around here.'

'And I am?'

'What?'

'From around here.'

'You know you are.'

'But I'm not your wife.'

'No, my wife is my wife. Do you understand? I am a man of the people. And apart from a little token exoticism which they enjoy, I have to reflect their beliefs and prejudices if I am to remain their blue-eyed boy. Therefore . . . Therefore, you have to allow me some leeway in whatever it is we have going. You know what I'm saying?'

'You're not seeing anyone else, are you?'

'Other than Jenny Lu?'

'Yes.'

'And you?'

'Yes.'

'No.'

'No?'

'The answer's no, sweetheart. On my soul. On the life of this government.'

'No?'

'Doesn't that make you happy?'

'I'm happy.'

'Then be glad you're happy.'

'But . . .'

'But what? What is it?'

'It's a sin, isn't it?'

'Sin? You think this is a sin? What we have. The wonderful beautiful natural thing we have, the feelings we share, you think this is a sin?'

'Sort of a sin.'

'Listen to me, sin is dead and gone, forget about sin, just try the best you can to do unto others, to love, and to, Jesus, Lorraine, this is not a fucking sin, don't you see that, this is a fucking backrub between friends, this is goodness, pure and simple, this is us being good people in a cruel world, caring and sharing and giving of ourselves, as the Lord God intended when he made us in his likeness with all our bits and bobs and our appetites and needs and cravings and God, your arse makes me want to shout for joy, you know that, sing hallelujah, praise the fucking Lord, don't you see why he made us like we are, he made us to be together, he made us to honour him and pour ourselves into love, into what he best intended, he gave us these bodies, he meant for us to use them, not to shamefully waste his gifts in gloom and guilt and wanking alone, making a cold dark lonely hell of our prime.'

'I don't know.'

'You're, not afraid of God?'

'God's God.'

'God's all-forgiving, there's no two ways around that, not that there's anything to forgive. Don't think for one second that God and me aren't hand-in-hand. You don't think I'd be where I am today if it wasn't for God being on my side. God is my right-hand man. He watches over me. And Lorraine, he watches over my friends. And you, Lorraine, you always have to bear in mind, you're a friend of Dave Foley and a friend of Dave Foley is a friend of God, fucking right.'

'My mother says . . .'

'Lorraine, for God's sake, leave your fucking shrivelled bitch rosary-thumping mother out of this.'

'She wants me to get married.'

'So get married.'

'But you're married and I want to marry you.'

'I've explained all that, haven't I, a fucking thousand times.'

'I love you.'

'And I love you. See, I'm not afraid to say it. And it's not just words with me. When I say it, I say it from the heart. I love you. I love you. I love you.'

'I want babies.'

'Jesus, now you're winding me up.'

'I'm ready to have babies. Don't you want babies?'

'You know me, I love babies, I love mothers, I love fucking everyone.'

'I want your babies.'

'Wait one minute, precious, one minute here. You're being careful, aren't you? I mean, you haven't stopped taking your little blue pills?'

'They're not blue.'

'Lorraine?'

'No. No, I haven't.'

'That's my girl. Now, listen, Lorraine. Are you listening?'

35

'They're pink.'

'*They're pink* is fine with me so long as they're doing the job the way God intended.'

'God?'

'He who watches over me.'

'But if, for instance, if say I missed a day or two by pure accident, an oversight, because sometimes I'm so tired and distracted I might forget, and then, and something happened, wouldn't that be God's way, doing what might be best for you and me?'

'That's one way of putting it and another way would be no matter how naive you appear, there's no chance of that happening, is there, because, it's simple really, the way things stand at the moment, the time is not right, anything along those lines would shag my standing at the polls and you wouldn't want that, now would you, would you?'

'I'm confused.'

'Yes, you are. But there's nothing wrong with being confused. We are all of us, the best of us, confused one time or another, but we don't let it get in our way, throw us off the path of our true destiny.'

'I have a destiny.'

'Destiny can be dangerous, you have to be careful where destiny's concerned. Destiny can drag you down. Destiny can degrade and vanquish you. You have to nurture destiny, mould it to your own purpose.'

'I pray for a baby. I pray to be married.'

'That's fine twenty years ago, darling, but these years, these are the, what do you call them, the zeros, the dawn of a new millennium, and frankly, that kind of baby-craving marriage-lust is wrong, all wrong, for the times in which we live.'

'Am I wicked then to want your baby?'

'You like working for me?'

'Yes.'

'A lot?'

'Very much.'

'Have I ever been less than a gentleman?'

'A gentleman?'

'Have I ever bawled you out in public, have I ever put my hand up your skirt when there were other people around?'

'No.'

'Is that a problem?'

'No.'

'Not that I don't want to put my hand up your skirt all the time, all day long, night and day, in front of the cabinet, the opposition, the press, the entire fucking nation, you understand, only . . .'

'You don't find me attractive enough to have babies with?'

'You're a lash.'

'I am?'

'You know you are. An outrageous fucking lash. Turns my heart to mush just to know you're here with me, so close, so kind, so tender, so devoted. An almighty fucking lash. The best.'

'That's nice of you to say so.'

'Think nothing of it.'

'If there's anything I can ever do for you.'

'I know that.'

'Now?'

'Why not?'

'I'll suck your peepee if you like.'

'Not at the moment, Lorraine, pet, please, nothing sexual for me, thank you.'

'I'll suck your toes?'

'My toes?'

'You tell me.'

'You want me to say it?'

'Say it.'

'Suck my toes.'

'Please.'

'Suck my toes, like a good girl. Please.'

'OK.'

'Hop to it.'

'Yes, sir.'

'And take your tits out while you're at it.'

'Oh, Dave.'

'You're the one, Lorraine, you're the one.'

Cats

When the light flickers we see the stamp in red postage due. Texas is wet with gripes. Yesterday it was cracked with them. Today it is wet with them. So it goes. There are no more ruses in the silos. The edge has dropped off. Some people have made the move to new houses in new neighborhoods as if it will succor them. It is so fragile. What stayed behind when they moved? What did they manage to shed? And what did they acquire? And did their cats travel with them? Three, I believe, they had, a stitched tom and two pussies, also. Also what? Stitched? Stitched cats do not like to capitulate. They would defy even time. They piss on prized shrubbery and edge their claws on priceless Louis Something furniture. Who gives a flying squid. The whole fabric is teetering anyhow and we are cutting cats and keeping them in our houses as if they were our allies and not vicious fifth columnists. Ours are getting so old they have lost the toilet habit of a lifetime spent in proximity to man and have taken to pooping on the stoop. It is painful to see. There is no other way of doing things, we will draw straws, Janet and I, and one of us will place the aged cats in a cardboard box and take them to a nearby field and use a shotgun on the box, the box so she will be saved from confronting her ignominy, whichever one of us it falls to. Civilization has crept up on us. What is there to be challenged by?

Distant landlocked vistas? Uranium in our water? No flowers please. Disposal of remains strictly private. Donations to usual charities. Our final meaning cannot be incontinence, must not be cack around our ankles when they find us dead in our sleep. We have said our goodbyes a thousand, thousand times. Our gentlemen callers are all dust and scattered.

Janet shot the young man when he climbed through the window. They say he was coming to check whether or not we'd taken too many pills and were already dead. We say he was coming through to abuse us or rob us. One or the other. Maybe both. Maybe he didn't deserve to die like that – face down in the cat litter – but all I can say is Janet was fully justified in her actions and that's an end to the matter. And besides, no young shaveneck whippersnapper in a store-bought suit is going to be fool enough to prosecute an old woman for protecting her property, her honor, at the end of her days, now is he? Not when he's sure as certain a publicity hound seeking election to higher office. Not when the authorities can't guarantee our well-being, not only on the streets but in our own homes, our girlhood homes.

Which is how come we keep a gun or two around the house, for the cats when their time comes. Lucky us, we say. Lucky us.

Catwalker

They get me to walk up and down. They get me to pout and strut. They get me to act horny. They get me to put on their clothes. They take my picture over and over and over. They put me in magazines and on TV and on billboards. They make me more and more famous. They try to understand my appeal. They ascribe frailties and illnesses to me. They put food in front of me and frown when I tuck in like a Southern girl. They watch me go in the restroom. They whisper cruel truths. They fuck me. They pay me. They give me things. They give me vacations. They give me jewelry. They give me fabulous wines. They give me drugs. They laugh at my jokes, especially my feeble ones. They empathize with my moods, my surliness, my manic petty tantrums. They think they're friends of mine. Everyone wants something. Even the mutant in the corner overlooks his very major mutant nature and views himself as fit to get from me some intimate token, some turgid sexual favor or other. It's a fucking circus.

Coffee With Mum

'I mean, what am I supposed to do, just because I'm forty . . .'
    'Fifty.'

'And separated. Lock myself away in this house the rest of my days until the Grim bloody Reaper comes a calling?'

'You could date him, see if he'd let you off in return for a very minor favour or two.'

'I don't see that you have to be so tart.'

'Just how old is he anyway, this Harry person?'

'Your age, thereabouts, give or take. Does it matter? Age, I mean.'

'What's he do?'

'Now don't be so suspicious.'

'You don't think he's after something?'

'Happiness. Love. Same as the rest of us.'

'Don't make me sick.'

'He works in the bank.'

'I knew it. They're all sneaky, greasy parasites.'

'I go in there all the time just to look at him. Three, four times a day. I feel like a girl again. I even write messages on the money I deposit. Round the edges of five-pound notes. *I love Harry Downey*. Sometimes in there, with all these other people standing around, and he's so close, I feel this intense urge to kiss him and when I can't, it gets so bad I almost faint, wishing I could lean across the counter and lick his eyes.'

'Mother. If you don't stop it I'm honestly going to be ill.'

'And you, are you seeing anyone special?'

'What do you think?'

'Anyone not special then?'

'No.'

'You know you don't have to live like a nun while you're waiting for the right man to come along.'

'I'm perfectly happy the way things are.'

'You meet men, don't you? Boys?'

'That's not the point.'

'You like men?'

'I'm not a lesbian, Mother.'

'So where's the difficulty?'

'Perhaps it's just that I have higher standards.'

'Than me? Oh, that's so funny.'

'I need to be sure before I embark on anything intimate.'

'Sure about what?'

'Myself.'

'You're young, attractive, healthy, clean.'

'Not that.'

'You are.'

'I mean I don't want to make mistakes.'

'The same mistakes as I make? Look, Jeannie, everyone makes mistakes. It's an intricate part of the plot.'

'Integral. I'm just not going to be another masochist, crying out for punishment.'

'I know what masochism means.'

'Who better.'

'What're you so afraid of? Sex isn't all bad.'

'You have this idea, don't you, that I'm a virgin or frigid or both?'

'You're telling me you're not? Well, I'm happy for you. Your father was a virgin, you know, when I first met him.'

'Jesus! Will you get it through your head, I'm not interested in hearing about your prehistoric mating rituals.'

'Prehistoric is a little harsh, don't you think?'

'It's all so icky and unsettling, not to mention tiresome.'

'Precisely how your father was between the sheets, why I had to throw him out in the end, and you know the hilarious thing is how everyone thinks he's the one who chucked me.'

'He was such a terrible lover, I wonder the dreadful experience didn't render you into some sort of man-hating, mate-phobic victim instead of this man-eating, menopausal merry-maker.'

'Man-eating, menopausal merry-maker? That's quite a mouthful, dear. You've been mulling over that one for some time, I can tell.'

'I should be going.'

'Have I really been such a dreadful role model?'

'Colourful. And it's not as if I ever had a choice, is it?'

'I only want what's best for you. Your father too.'

'I can't be you, either of you.'

'No one expects you to be.'

'Tell me the truth. When you look at me, don't you wonder where things have gone wrong on the charm and libido front, why I haven't inherited any of Dad's, I hate to use the word charisma, or for that matter any of your sexual allure or moral abandon?'

'I love you.'

'That doesn't count. Look, it's OK, I've always known I'll never meet your expectations.'

'No. You speak so well. I'm so proud of you.'

'Really?'

'With parents like you've had, I'm amazed you're such a wonderful child.'

'I'm not a child. And most of the time I'm suicidal.'

'You're my child. And you're not suicidal. You're high-feeling. And when you finally find your niche in life, I'm sure you'll be the most fulfilled happy creature.'

'Mother, I didn't mean anything harsh I might have said just now.'

'I know, dear. Now, do you need anything?'

'I'm fine.'

'You only have to ask.'

'Thank you. Honestly. I'm fine.'

Cravings

The blue beyond is here and now. That's a brilliant notion. I honestly think that. I'm twenty-five. Still standing. This town is tired. This life. This body. The baby is greedy. She grows more and more greedy and selfish with each passing hour. She grows stronger as I grow more weary. Her life cuts through mine. Cuts me in half. Half today. More tomorrow. Until there's less and less of me remaining. The fact of her being sometimes hits me like a fever, makes me delirious, sends me out in a frenzy to provide, to prove our lives are real and worthwhile, to secure them for another day, another week, another month. This sort of euphoria keeps me speeding along for a while. Then it goes and I'm left by myself. Emptied once more. But with time, the strong feeling returns. Always returns. Like a craving for fruit or chocolate or the press of human flesh.

Daughters

My brother Gene intimated to me that it might be a blessing were I to remember less, while I thought my problem centered on the fact that I couldn't remember enough, well enough. There have been escapades, scrapes enough in my time, but somehow all of that's muddled. I say you don't get to be middle-aged without logging some mileage. The time I talked myself into walking out on Sam and bringing Sarah and Susan home to Mother just because I was horrified and restive to be thirty-five, unadored and untouched – at the time I hadn't let Sam near me in over two years. One thing always puzzled me was how he was so patient. How did his staying away from me reflect on me, my attractiveness? Or perhaps, more to the point, had he girlfriends who made up for my coldness, I hesitate to use the term 'frigidity', or did he perhaps patronize prostitutes during that time? I was loud, I guess, when I was a girl, and free, or so I thought, to get away with all sorts of horseplay and high spirits. There were always boys around to go riding cross-country with. Boys to get flirty with. And fire off their daddies' guns with into the empty night. Boys to wrestle with. Boys to fish the Green River with and have them take me rafting. You had to be skillful and fearless to cut through the gorges back of Moab and the ones who made it I believed I could trust and felt obliged to let them go all the way if they'd expressed an interest, which most of them had. Then when I went back East to college there were swisher boys to show me around Europe and one long summer there was Mexico and Guatemala and the boys I traveled down with and the boys I found there waiting for me. Always returning to hometown boys grown taller and leaner. And some of them meaner. And some of them hungrier. Boys to go to church with. Boys to stay out all night with. Dangerous boys, and wild and crazy boys, and shy ones. And ride in their brothers' borrowed trucks with down bone-shaking back roads, shrouding ourselves inside and out with that fine powder dust I'd taste for weeks after, coming back to startle me while I'd be kissing some other clean-shirted boy in some far-off city. Boys to drink illicit whiskey with. Boys to start a fight with for no good reason, shoving and punching and kicking them until they can't take it and suddenly they're boys to get thrown to the ground by and then standing over me, all out of breath and ashamed and just about to cry for what they hadn't meant to do, they're boys to laugh at. Boys to whisper secrets to and dreams and hurts and jealousies. Boys to take by the hand. Boys to stand out in the rain with. Until one day you wake up and you wonder where the boys are gone, where the barns are where the boys used to take out their things, petulant things you had to kneel to. Now I have daughters I wonder what they'll have to remember in thirty years' time. Daughters, I said to Gene, no one knows what it's like to have daughters. And he said, Sure, you know such a hell of a lot about it yourself.

Drive-by

It's like around the time G's been gone a few weeks and one night it's late and I'm just riding around with an ache in my chest and I think I see her car outside a late-night grocery store so I turn in and drive over and find I'm right, it is her humble old rumbling green-chipped seventies Mustang Ghia, a car she keeps to show how success hasn't turned her head, no matter that she always had money, grew up easy, was always used to better things, better cars than old sun-faded, nothing-special Mustangs, so I park and go inside and sure enough she's there, my G, and at first I don't go up to her or anything, I just follow her around, trying not to let her see me, she's so beautiful, she gleams, she's wearing shades and a blue sleeveless top and a khaki cottony skirt to her knees and bare legs and rippled blue, wedged Nike Air Rift sneakers with no socks and her honey-colored hair's in a stray sort of tied-up way with wispy bits escaping like I love and she's really focused like always, plucking items from shelves, moving along relentlessly, grimly, under some tight personal schedule, and then I can't hardly breathe, I think I'm having some sort of attack, you know, and I clutch at this shelving and knock over a jar of something, I don't even notice what it is, and she sees me, and I'm not lurking anymore, I mean I'm still finding it hard to catch my breath and I'm feeling a little foolish and ashamed like I've been caught snooping, like I'm just another wannabe starfucker off the street, and she comes storming over, pushing her shopping cart in front of her, crashing it against my legs, and I yelp and hop away, and she pushes after me, hemming me in, trapping me against some more shelving and she goes, mad as hell, 'What are you doing here, you asshole?' and I feel like backing off, I can't hardly speak or swallow or even look at her, and she pursues me, nudging me all the time with the cart, going, 'You think you can sneak up on me, picking up the pieces? God, what is this!' and I go, all pathetic, 'I wish,' and she shakes her head contemptuously and pushes past me, and I'm still going, 'I wish,' and then, I can't explain it, I sheepishly shuffle after her, saying, 'You look great,' and I pick a grapefruit from her cart and go, 'Eating all the right things, that's good,' and she snatches back the grapefruit, tosses it in her cart, keeps moving on down the aisle with me following and I go, 'Maybe I could ask you something? it doesn't matter really, it's just you look so wonderful and everything and I can't help wondering,' and she snaps at me, 'What?' and I go in this hushed voice, 'What do you weigh now?' which is certainly the wrong thing to say in the circumstances because she turns on me and demands in her most explosive way, 'What do you mean what do I weigh now?' and I'm alarmed, I mean I don't want to annoy her or upset her, you know, that's the last thing I want, and I say to her, I say, 'Nothing, nothing, forget I ever,' and she cuts me off, going, 'Look, you, I'm not pregnant, I never said I was pregnant, in fact I think I should have told you before but I don't think I can ever have kids,' and right then I don't know what to think, I'm bereft, truly bereft, and I go, 'G, honey, don't talk like that,' and she goes back at me, 'Can't you please leave me alone?' and I shake my head, and this must be my weakness but I know I can't let go, never will, and she makes this pleading, extremely cross face and she goes, 'Try,' and she moves away again and I trot after her, I'm so pathetic, I know, saying, all sort of whiney, 'It's not over, G, it's not over,' and she goes, like once-and-for-all, she goes, 'Look, there's only one of me and I don't feel like being agreeable right now,' and I go, as agreeably as I can, I go, 'You don't feel like being agreeable, I don't feel like being agreeable, we should be happy together,' and she frowns at me, going, 'Christ, you're really not getting the picture, are you?' and I give her a big smile and hug her awkwardly, and go, 'Pretty, pretty, G,' and she moves uncomfortably in my arms, her head banging against my face, sort of going out of her way I think to show, you know, that we don't fit together, and then, it's a bit of a surprise really, there's this sudden immense flood of tears from her, gushing, and she goes, 'You say that like,' and I go, 'Don't cry,' and she goes, sobbing, 'As if pretty's all there is to me,' and I go, 'Don't cry,' and she goes, 'Drop dead,' and pushes me away, and I plead, going, 'G, G,' and she goes, 'It's how you see me, isn't it, having a job with a hairdressing allowance?' and even though, you know, she has, the whole world knows she has, it's part of the package, and I go, 'I'm just saying,' and she goes, 'Always just saying, always pressing the same view, ignoring the facts, talking to my ass,' and I don't know why but I snap, I've taken so much grief the last couple of weeks, the rumors, the snide remarks suggesting my career needs us to be a couple, which isn't fair or true, you know, because I had a career long before she came along, I go, 'You women, you're all the same,' and she goes, 'Buster,' and steps up to me and punches me full on the mouth, and I'm stunned, you can imagine, because it's not a stunt this time, it's real, the power, man, in her skinny little fist, it's really something, and it hits me doubly, you know, the realization, the fact she didn't give a fuck it was my face she was hitting, my career she was threatening, then I realize there's blood dripping from my mouth so I have to bend over to let it flow to the tiled floor, and I go, 'Why'd you pop me? why'd you do that? do you like it acting tough or what?' and she grabs a pack of peas from a freezer display and shoves it hard against my face, and she goes, softly, 'Why can't you get one thing right, why can't you leave me alone,' and then she drops the pack of peas and tilts my head to check on the bleeding, and dabs at my burst lip with a fold of warm Kleenex she takes from her pocket, and I'm starting to feel good and confident again, you know, close to her, so I go, in a humorous way, 'I'll be God to you,' and she frowns, not seeing the funny side of it, and I root out a giant chocolate bar from her cart, and go, like after all, 'You missed me, didn't you?' and she goes, 'Fuck you,' and rams me right in the crotch with the cart, this time sending me crashing backward into an open-topped freezer and I lie there unmoving, surrounded by packets of frozen foods, vegetables, Wolfgang Puck's and Birds Eye and Von's own brand, and she reaches in and shakes me and I don't revive, I don't want to, I want her to feel sorry, sorry for what she's done, sorry for me, sorry for everything, the broken promise of our love, our lost future together, that sort of thing, and she clutches me to her, her soft warm front, her scent, it's all I ever dream of, and she doesn't have a bra on, and I open my eyes and smile, so fucking unbelievably content in her embrace, it's like old times with her nursing me, and like, my hands start roaming over her shoulders in a really natural way and she stiffens and goes, 'What am I doing?' and she lets go of me, drops me back in the freezer and walks away and by the time I lean up out of there, all hoary and frosted it feels like, she's way down by the checkouts, so I climb out of there fairly smartly, bumping my mouth in the process so it starts the bleeding again, and I press a pack of frozen something yellow, corn maybe, to where it's bleeding and hurry down there after her, and go, mumbling through the corn, the cold plastic packing, 'G, don't do this to me,' and she goes, right there in front of the bored checkout girl, this hot-looking Mexican kid, who doesn't seem to recognize either of us, maybe she doesn't have a TV or go to the movies or read the rags, or maybe she just can't see past the corn, and G goes, not under her breath at all like maybe you'd think she would if she wanted to stay anonymous and keep our little tiff under wraps, 'You and your kisses and smiles, your whole little sick repertoire,' and I go, 'G, baby,' sort of thinking about the checkout girl, checking her out, you know, if maybe she's interested in me or maybe she's appalled or possibly turned on by my bloody face, who knows with women, there's blood on my shirt, pretty much everywhere, I'm not looking my best, OK, and G, she goes, 'Lies, lies,' and I honestly don't know what she means by lies in this instance, she just turns and walks away, abandons her shopping, abandons the checkout girl, abandons me, abandons our future together, and I can't let it all end like this, can I? so I rush after her, only see, this vigilant slick of a trainee manager spots me trying to leave with the pack of frozen corn still in my hand and he hurries to cut me off, crying out, 'Mister, Mister, where you going with my *Hungry Man* vegetable?' and I can see G outside, striding away toward the parking lot, and this mad son of a bitch grabs me and there's a bit of a scuffle and he's really strong, you know, monster strong, must come from all those years stacking shelves, and he pins me to the big window at the front, so my face is pressed up against the glass and he's got me in this stranglehold, and he's calling to the checkout girl to call security, Magdalena he calls her, and I can picture the messy headlines, the *National Enquirer* apoplexy at more movie-brat outrage against the small decent people, not a word about how this clown's preventing me from going after G, catching up to her, the woman I love, the woman a million other guys want to pork, I mean, get in line, I'm at the head of that particular line, always, and this is his big opportunity, Mr Stacker-Of-The-Month, denying me my destiny, making a name for himself, using altogether unnecessary roughness, keeping me crushed against the window, honestly, it's raw folly, and he so over-the-top righteously snatches the bloody packet of corn away from me, like he's just nabbed a Ten-Most-Wanted psycho-hoodlum, you know, and G's car goes by, and she doesn't look in my direction or anything, she just drives on by, and I start worrying that this is going to be the last time I see her, this is going to be how she remembers me, and then that Magdalena comes over and gives me this shy half-smile and I see how stacked she is, a stunner in her nylon bib and cheap makeup, and I think there's consolations in this life if not much hope.

Flight

I turn and turn that last night, unable to sleep, unable to breathe, unable to go, unable to stay. Finally, when I do sleep, I dream that someone lies dead in my bed and I have no idea who it is, what they ever did to me, or meant to me, if anything. Five a.m. I'm awake and up, worrying all the time whether this is the right decision, and if it isn't, if it's the wrong choice then things will never be the same again. Lean into the mirror. Teeth intact. No more bruises. Only a little puffiness under the eyes. Think what collagen treatment would do for me around my mouth; Botox; the cracks appearing daily, deepening each time I look into a glass. Rush to get packed, coffeed, showered, blow-dried, made-up, lenses applied, and, finally, dressed. Matching deeply russet underwear, black ribbed rollneck sweater, black jacket, red tartan above-the-knee skirt, black opaque hose, black pumps. Gold chain necklace, Chopard wristwatch with diamonds set on the glass and ruby shoulders, five rings on four fingers, charm bracelet, blank link bracelet, earrings. And in my bag (Prada alligator; a gift from Stanley; $5,000 retail): passport, driver's license, ticket, datebook and pen, Visa, AmEx, Diner's, Mastercard, cash, coins, keys, lens case, glasses, sunglasses, tissues, absurdly token tampon, cologne, compact, comb, lipgloss, mascara, eyeliner pencil, moisturizer, mints. I feel rushed, as if I'm missing some final detail; forgetting something essential. I feel like I did at fourteen: unreal and untrue; alien; enviously hovering while everyone else was involved or possessed. I look around the room. The bed unmade. The closets achingly laden. Shoes and hangers and towels and hairbrush and stockings scattered across the bed and floor. The prevailing scent one of Lancôme's. A last check in the cheval glass. I notice my hands. They seem so composed and exquisitely formed, as if they're not mine, as if they're idealized, cadaverous, dead and dumb from an Ingres or a Sargent portrait. And then it's time to go, to leave all this behind.

Football

One day I woke up to find I was married. It wasn't a career move. And it certainly wasn't anything to do with sex or love or romance or any of that. And it wasn't to do with a desire for affection or companionship or even security. I think mostly it had to do with football. Because Newcomb was a footballer. And football was suddenly hot. Andy Newcomb was his name. And I was Mrs Andy Newcomb. For a very short forgettable while. Though I do remember that he drove a black Porsche. He was an OK driver. And he had a big house in Cheshire from when he used to play for another club up north and he talked about retiring there and breeding a new generation of superior footballers. That certainly buttered me. Despite not having what you'd call hips, you only have to look at me to see I'm the maternal type.

Fucking Bicycles

Only this morning, I'm cycling to work when something goes wrong with the bike and I get off to find the chain's all snagged and grotty, and I get so frustrated, and what do I do, I throw the bike right in this hedge and just stand there for ages until I realise this isn't going to resolve anything, never mind get me in to work on time, so I retrieve the bike, walk off, pushing it, thinking God help any man crosses my path. Pricks. Responsible for the woes of the world. Herpes. Fucking bicycles.

Girlfriend

I'm fasting to make myself even more desirable, even more worthy of his devotion, guarantee he'll stay eternally mine. Sneak a salty cream cracker and a glass of boiled tap water mid-morning. Lunchtime, rush out to meet with loyal and faithful girlfriend in the park. She's in a sour mood and forces herself to consume a messy designer sandwich as if to rebuke and deny all societal-cum-peer pressure to conform and be svelte. I avert my eyes and sip from a bottle of obscure Pyrenean mineral water, the taste for which is a souvenir of last month's uneventful Andorran skiing holiday . . . not a hint of a viable man in thirteen long days and nights, only swarms of pale-eyed, off-piste showboaters and opportunistic love hounds.

'I never thought,' I say, 'the day would come but I think he's the one.'

'How can you be sure?'

'I puked in his lap and he never batted an eyelid.'

'What's that mean? It might just be he has the constitution of a dog.'

I give this notion a moment's consideration and dismiss it. 'It was chicken vindaloo, and sweet and sour pork, and five pints of cider. Buckets and buckets of golden steaming puke.'

My devoted girlfriend regards her designer sandwich with unease and drops it on the patchy grass behind the bench.

'I think it's time I checked him out,' she says.

A mangy pigeon moves in to peck at the discarded sandwich. A pitiful specimen with groggy movements, ruffled feathers and sundry growths flowering on its alopecic head, unhappily reminds us of innumerable suitors. Embarrassed by its doomed appearance we silently get to our feet and leave the bird to dine in peace. How they all used to clamour to gorge on us. Their vain pricks, so flighty and inconstant.

Gone Fishing

I think about where I can get away to. Somewhere quiet. Somewhere warm. Madeira would be nice. I remember the hotel gardens there. I remember being on a boat, a small boat, rising and falling on the heavy swell, with Garret, my boss, alongside me, reeling in an ocean-dwelling monster, *Xiphias gladius* by the book is what he told me, swordfish in close-up dauntless reality, until both he and the fish were exhausted and seemed to be one. I remember how the sun beat down on the cobalt sea, dazzling, freckling my shoulders. The boatman towed the swordfish through the water to revive it before releasing it. Otherwise it would have sunk to the depths and perished. I rubbed Garret's shoulders, easing away the strain, the afterburn of so much expended effort, and he talked about it being a day to remember. I kissed and kissed him then with all my warmth, straining to make him see how much I felt for him. And later that night, after dinner, back in his hotel room, we made love, rapturous carefree love. The out of doors awash with moonlight, accompanied by the plaint of wind chimes which a pest of a child had hung from another balcony. And then the phone rang and I held my breath and listened while he talked to his wife for twenty minutes. And then I went to sleep and dreamed I was under the sea with the swordfish, free and easy, with no one hunting me, with no idea of love to haunt me.

Goosebumps

It's Cameron. He wants to see me. I don't let him know how happy I am that he's called. Though I didn't leave him with much choice, did I. Considering he's a man and I'm . . . What am I exactly? So I go wait for him in the park, stretch out on the grass, a book over my face. I can tell when he walks through the gates, my skin goes practically goosebumped while he's still a hundred yards away. I don't move, I don't raise my head or turn my eyes to look in his direction. I play it cool. He walks right up beside me. I can hear his breathing. He says nothing. I know he's looking down at me, running his eyes over me. Finally, enough of the free show, I remove the book from my face, shade my eyes, look up at him. 'I didn't think you'd come,' he says. 'I see you brought your ball,' I say. It's an orange plastic regulation size with the price sticker still on. £1.99, it says. He holds out his hand and pulls me upright. Then we go play football. Any chance I get I kick him. Finally, he grabs me and puts me over his shoulder and takes me back to my place to ravage me. And then I ravage him. And then he devours me. And then . . . well, what I find is, if you're not personally involved, it gets so very tedious and frustrating to have to hear every last devouring detail of someone else's happy clinches . . . So, tell me, how are things with you? But first, I have to tell you, after a couple of hours, I'm getting this burn from his beard, I need a break, I send him to the shops for wine and biscuits and a razor and he comes back additionally with two red plastic water pistols which he fills with wine and we fly through half a bottle, shooting each other in the mouth. After he's shaved we engage in this mock serious debate about the morality of allowing any guns whatsoever in the house . . . 'I won't have them,' I say . . . but he takes up the front of my blouse and whispers to my belly some persuasive argument to do with rearming and resisting appeasement and his breath begins to tickle so I ditch my moral qualms, they go right out the window, and over the next two days we fuck like fifteen different ways, like we've never fucked before, like we'll never fuck again.

Hangdog

The wind came down from out of those frozen godforsaken hills, funneled faster every yard it came, every foot it sank along the valley, perishing the sense from all, even those that clung to nothing more than perdition. Frank came home from town and a long day at the mart and, somewhere between too many beers and too few, found his gun dog, Blackpaw, he'd paid his brother-in-law, Duxie, three hundred pounds for, getting serviced by what he could only term a pussy runt hippie terrier. So Frank, he bent over and caught up a frozen clod of dirt and grass and ice and flung it with a curdling roar at the grotesquely welded canines. The pussy runt glanced Frank's way and took off for the bog, it was all bog up there, that dog was gone, never to be seen again. Blackpaw, a sort of short-haired German bird dog masquerading sometimes, depending on the sentimental veil descended on her master when he was tight or stoned, as a springer spaniel, came bellying over to lie by Frank's insulated Drinagh Co-op-bought boots manufactured in Romania and no denying that cheap pedigree, God blast that treachery he was obliged by Brussels-imposed retail strictures to walk around in, his toes half-rot with frost one minute, damp the next, and that way never evade. Frank produced a smile and crouched to fondle the scruff of the disappointing mutt. I can help you, said Frank, you mutinous bitch. The dog seemed to smile, you'd certainly think it the way its mouth came open and its pink tongue fell shamelessly out. Frank stood then and hauled the dog across the frozen yard and kicked open the stable door so it swung back and clattered off the wall of railway sleepers and hung there lopsided on one rusted loose butt hinge while Frank cast about for a rope and keeping the shivering dog between his knees he quickly fashioned a noose and collared the dog and fed the line through an iron hoop fixed in a roof beam, stood away and hauled on that line until the dog rose off its hinderquarters and struggled there, searching desperate and foolish the air, as if that medium ever offered purchase. Frank pulled some more and the dog rose some more. And then the dog gave over struggling and its tongue dangled grotesque and its piss and scutter came forth and Frank hung on another while and then he let go the line and the faithless dog fell to the frozen hard floor. He spat then and wiped his hands on his dirt-caked jeans and walked over to lift the noose from the dog's neck and slip it over its head. He threw the rope away in a corner raked high with clotted straw. He walked to get the door. That Duxie, thought Frank, selling him a nothing dog like this. So long, said Frank, pulling the door shut but not before he felt the spirit of the dead dog slip out and away into those dark empty hills. Frank knew from thirty-five years of the shit what it was all about. You always either get or give it. No two ways. That dog, Frank's deed, might haunt another soul, not Frank. Frank bought it years later. Coming home roaring drunk from town one night he'd run off the road. A road he'd ridden a thousand times with hardly a scrape. Not this night. He rolled her over. The car burned out, did Frank to a crisp. No one shed a tear. No one heard a dog howl. I thought they might. Later, I bought one of Frank's guns off his sister's husband, Duxie. Cut from the same cloth they were, only Duxie's not dead yet. Bastarding tightass mutant mean hungry fucker. One day maybe, one day.

His Bergman Phase

After six months with Cees, it's very strange, I find myself listening to myself, being very aware that I'm starting to sound as if English is not my mother tongue. Then the next thing I know, he's sending me home, we're standing in Schipol with him having no more to do with me, telling me I'm impossible, telling me he hates all Irish girls, will have no more to do with them or me or anyone only big blonde busty Lowlanders with butter-churning biceps and lips that taste of wild raspberries. I have no idea what he meant only think maybe he was going through a Bergman phase at the time. Probably still is. Bloody Lutherans.

Ice Cream

'Billy,' I say.

He looks at me.

'Maybe,' I say, 'maybe you'd get us something.'

'We don't have time now,' he says.

It's a relief to hear his voice. Like I must have been dreading he'd never speak to me again. But now I know he's still with me.

'Some ice cream maybe,' I say.

He looks at me like he can't tell what's in my mind. I lower my head, drop my chin on my chest and wish we could go back. I wish none of this had ever happened.

First, though, Billy stops the car and reverses back up the street and into the parking lot of this store which is still open at this late hour and all lit up and he smiles at me, wanting me to be happy about something, anything, and we get out and walk to the store and the automatic doors glide open and Muzak bleeds into the night and we step inside and the doors close and anyone left outside in the night would be deprived of the sweet Muzak and cool air and wouldn't be able to smell us the way we smell which is young and pure and trembling.

A disembodied voice speaks to us like we're the most important people in the world, drawing us further and deeper into the store, telling us about all the bargains on offer and Billy grabs a shopping cart and starts pushing it, leaning over on the push-bar like some lanky hero out of the old West, if he only had a match between his teeth, only he pays no heed to the produce he passes and I just go along with him. In his wake. I'm happy. Looking at all that's on offer. Then I'm in the toiletries section by myself and it's all a mystery. I see my bruised face reflected in a mirror-clad display stand. I look at the mystifying array of cosmetics. I spot a rack of sunglasses and hurry over. I try on a pair. I check them out in a mirror. I try on another pair and check them. And another. Hamming it a bit this time. More and more. I try a fourth and fifth and sixth and seventh pair and these last ones, these, I decide, are the ones for me, as well as seven being my lucky number. And making this decision is the best feeling I've had in ages even though I know maybe I don't look all that wonderful really. I spin the display until I find a matching pair and go off to find Billy. I spot him lazing, drifting across the end of the aisle ahead of me. I hurry after him and scoot round the corner only to find a young blond woman all immaculate and glamorous right there in my way. I don't know where she's from, where she's come from tonight, she doesn't look like she belongs here. She wears shades but like she deserves to, like she's born to it and entitled like I can never be. She plucks produce from the shelves like she has money enough to buy out the whole place in one shot, like she knows what all these jars and tubs contain and how you're supposed to cook them and eat them and everything. She moves on. Wound-up. Pretty and grim. Under some strain of her own. I can tell she's not happy. She glances at me. I don't mean nothing to her. I don't register. She goes on. I find Billy. I give him the shades I got for him. He rips off the tag and puts them on. He gives me a big old grin and that's nice. We look like we're together. We're not raw or twitchy anymore. We walk to where the ice cream is and he boots that empty cart he's been lugging around, sends it skating away, loudly crashing into glass-fronted freezer cases and he picks me out a big tub of vanilla and we walk straight and tall right to the checkout, the big tub of ice cream shoved up under Billy's shirt, freezing against his bare skin, and we're walking through, him first, then me, but close enough so I can reach out and touch his shirt if I need to, just walking through like we've nothing to pay for, like we've found nothing in this entire retail wonderland to appeal to us, and no one stops us, no one comes after us.

Indifference

Indifference kills me. Lie. The folds and bloom of my sex deny nothing. I prove to myself I am the way. I open myself to fate and fortune. The weight of a man, a stranger in my arms, does not oppress me. Men are insubstantial. I close my eyes and float away. The man may find himself in a blind alley, desperate for light or sustenance or validation, craving achievement or even affection. That is nothing to me. That is not my responsibility. That is not my doing. Each of us makes our own way in the world. I lead myself. I provide for myself and my child. You don't know me. No one knows me. Not even the child knows me. Nor the mother that bore me. Nor the man that married me. But I know you. I know how easy it is to distract you. I know how easy it is to infuriate and enrage you. But still you want to know me. And for one reason only. To finish with me. To get to the end of me. To process me with your little minds. And then to shit me out. That's the way it is. Always the same.

In The Limo With S

Aaron, he's my agent now, he saw me on TV and called me up, asking whether I'd ever considered being a writer and writing, you know, a book. A book? I said. A book, he said. Would you like me to suck your cock! I said. No! I never! I'm only joking. I didn't have to. I mean, it wasn't expected and if it was, I'm not that sort of girl. So I asked him what sort of book he had in mind. Anything you like, he said. And I thought long and hard, you know, because I didn't want it to be like

Naomi's book although that sold a lot, didn't it? Naomi's such a clever sweet girl, I love her to bits, do you know her? So right away I remembered how much I know about international relations so that's what I wrote about. International relations. Sex and drugs and money in the glitz glam world of couture. So I packed in the modelling and started writing. And everything's been a dream since then. Everybody's been so generous and kind and really, you know, supportive, completely supportive. I wrote the thing in a rush, three hundred pages in three weeks, and was launched and everything in no time. Don't you love the jacket photo? I don't think I look that hot in real life, do I? Thank you, you're so sweet. Yes, I wrote it all myself. I used one of those, what do you call them, like tape recorders. I mean, one of those really really small ones. They're so clever, aren't they, the way they keep making everything smaller. Oh, you've one in your pocket. Isn't it sweet. They couldn't stop me talking in it. I made boxes and boxes of tapes. In the end they had to take it away from me, I think I'd still be writing if they hadn't, you know, because I simply had so much more to say. Tons and tons of terrific stuff. What's that? Oh, no, I'm sorry, I'm not supposed to tell how much the advance was. Well, OK, it was three hundred and thirty-three thousand, three hundred and thirty-three pounds and thirty-three pence. Nice, isn't it, the way all the threes sort of come together. Am I happy? Definitely, yes, mostly, yes, absolutely. The book is selling. And I love New York, don't you. Sometimes maybe I do feel a little lonely. Am I talking too much? Of course I miss modelling. Plus a lot of other things. Milan. Paris. The shows. But I still have my friends, my family, my dogs, whenever I get home. I love my dogs. I don't really take the threats on my life seriously. I mean, if Salman Rushdie can do it, I can. It's just a tiny proportion of people can't cope when they see someone else being successful, letting her talent flourish. They just have to bitch, you know, they don't need an excuse or anything. They're just like professional bitches. Negative, negative people. And, I mean, that rebounds, doesn't it. Eventually. I mean, personally I take a karmic view of things like life and stuff. Would you like me to do anything for you? I won't be offended if you're not interested. You're German, aren't you? I mean, who am I? I'm just a wee Scottish girl. I'm nobody. OK, maybe I did write a best-seller, but what does that really mean in the overall run of things? Not a lot. I'm sure you're a wonderful writer. You look like you are. You do. You don't know a Christophe, do you? He took my picture once for German *Vogue*? No, I'm wrong, he's Austrian. That's not the same thing at all, is it? The driver? He's OK. Why don't you slide over here. No, don't kiss me. Here, give me your hand. Oh, yes, that's nice. What'd you say your name was? Dietrich? Dieter? Dieter, is that it? Dieter. No, don't stop. What about Maggie Rizer? People are always saying that to me. But I don't see it. I don't think I look at all like her. I mean, she's not Scottish, is she. And anyway I'm me. Plus I was around before her, you know. Not long before her, but before her. So, if anything, and I honestly don't think it for a moment, she's the one looks like me and not the other way round. Right? I know it's the freckles maybe. It's just I'm sick of the freckles, OK. I don't know what's the big deal about a few freckles. Sometimes I look in the mirror and wish I were coloured, you know, like a black girl. Do black people have freckles? I don't think so. Yes, how's that? OK? Do you like that? Why don't you go right ahead and . . . Oh, Dieter, oh, you poor darling. Don't apologise. Look, it's all my fault, nattering on. I know it's distracting. I'm so sorry. I'm such a chatty cow. No, *chatty*. Chitty Chitty Bang Bang is something else. Chitty, yes, ch-ch. There's some Kleenex in the what-do-you-call-it, yes, in there. Stop worrying. Of course it'll come out. It always comes out. You know, I don't think I've ever been in a city with more dry-cleaners. There's practically one on every street corner. I don't think Maggie Rizer is that pretty. I mean, she has a sort of freak quality to her which she exploits, doesn't she. Classical beauty is another matter. Classical beauty endures through all the fads and fashions. No, I'm not saying I think she's unattractive. Why do you care about her anyway? I mean, you're beginning to sound like you've a bit of a hang-up where she's concerned. Which is really rather rude and inconsiderate of you when you're here with me, riding around with me in my limo. I mean, you don't see Maggie Rizer in here anywhere, do you, so fuck it, I don't see why we have to spend the entire night talking about her. No, you don't have to apologise. Do I look all right? I mean, I feel like I'm coming down with something. It's like the start of something. Yes, a little fevered. And some migraine. And light-headed. It's probably just one of those twenty-four-hour bugs. Yes, that could be it, you're right, it's something I ate. Oh, would you? You wouldn't mind? Maybe that would be for the best. I hope you don't think I'm throwing you out or anything. I adored chatting with you. And I want you to remember me well and write something terribly, terribly nice about me. Promise? Just tap on the window and tell him you feel like walking. I'm fine. Honestly. Good night. Ciao to you too.

Jellied Eels

Of course Matthew's getting himself into my bed is not an instant effortless achievement on his part. It takes time. He has to woo me. Our first date, he establishes his credentials: thirty-four next birthday which means he's the age of Christ (I'm having to put from my mind all thoughts of what it would be like to dawdle with Jesus); clear-pored; 6'2" in his socks; size eleven shoe; circumcised (I never ask; it comes up; he volunteers; no big issue; how blasé as a society are we regarding male mutilation when we all get huffy regarding female equivalent, rightly icksome); a first from Cambridge; an MBA from Northwestern, which is in or near Chicago, I don't want to reveal my ignorance by asking precisely where it is; he earns, I estimate, no more than a moderately talented Nationwide League player such as Ipswich's Kenny McE— whom I lunched and interviewed a few weeks ago for *FourFourTwo* – £180 + lunch + train – maybe four thousand a week ballpark for dressing as a banker and sitting at a desk, advising entrepreneurs how to be more shark-like, fend off the onslaught of government, Brussels and the burgeoning Albanian Mafyia; was once almost engaged to a lovely soul called Clarissa who later tragically lost her life three-day eventing; drives a Porsche Carrera 911; dances; loves kids, his sister has two, Chubb and Bunty, he wants four; scuba-dives; just back from the Red Sea; golfs off a five handicap; allows Roy Keane is both pivotal and inspirational to Man Utd; enjoys nothing more than flying out to Marbella for the weekend to stay at his family's three-hundred-acre *finca* with vines, olive trees, cork oaks, a year-round outdoor pool, all you could ask of a *finca*, really. All of which –

the property, the footballer's wage, the smile, the vanished foreskin – should make me weak-kneed, but doesn't. Of course what if he were Matt rather than Matthew, had a flat nose, and earned his living in the Nationwide like Kenny McE—? That would make him what? A catch? Dateable? Maybe if he were ten years younger, ten years at ten to fifteen thousand a week, that'd give him a certain cachet, make some girls certainly give him a second glance. But a banker is a different kettle of fish. I mean, it's not as if he's a doctor which as every girl knows is marginally better than his being a footballer. He's looking at me like he knows I've been doing my sums. I reach out and stroke the sleeve of his suit jacket, consoling him, as if he needs consoling. He laughs. Shows his big white teeth. They've been fixed. Definitely. Capped and bleached. Suggests either a dental disaster zone or a youth given over to some contact sport or other. Probably rugby union. This is a watershed moment for me. And I hate to admit it but I'm charmed to the point of being pixilated. The clincher comes when he shows a capacity for self-mockery by taking me pitch-and-putting out by Epping Forest which leads to hands on hips for illustrative purposes alone initially, warm breath in ears, calling me Bellingham instead of Eugenie, which is oddly exciting, and so forth. Not forgetting a protracted lunch of warm beer, jellied eel, pasties and a moderately sized gherkin apiece. After which it seems churlish not to acknowledge our mutual attraction and postpone any longer the inevitable shag by old hat Jane Austeny, Bridget Jonesy misunderstandings, shallow conflict, faux prudery, or indeed lunch-induced halitosis. Turns out he's quite keen and capable in bed and once that rolling around, panting and sweating and striving for bliss business is done with – I gave all the usual encouraging signs, squealing, flapping and crying, maybe more of a high-pitched urgency than was warranted by his dutiful, essentially unimaginative, regard for my pleasure, yes, he was there for me – we press ahead with getting to know one another. Carnal duties done, he rolls away from me, and I get down to brassy essentials, asking, apropos my recent appearance on a non-terrestrial television football show, 'What did you really think when you saw me on TV? No, don't tell me. Was I rabid?'

'Very much.'

'Oh, Christ. I knew it.'

'It was . . .'

'Don't say refreshing. Please don't.'

'How about interesting?'

'Interesting in a fruit sort of way, sweaty and manic and twitchy limbs, and a horrible old cardie with cat hairs all over, or interesting as a big old crazed heifer in a china store or a vault full of Meissen figurines?'

He's stopped what he was doing, scratching some part of his nether regions, and seems to be appraising me afresh, captivated no doubt by my loopy nature. And out of the blue . . . totally unwarranted, I mean I think I can truthfully claim that in the short time I've known him I never consciously led him on or encouraged him to go the ultimate distance, never imagined my hold on him was anything more than fleeting . . . what's he come out with only, 'Bellingham, I want you to meet my people.'

'Your people?'

'My mother.'

His mother? Honestly. I don't know whether to laugh or cry.

He's serious all right. He presses on, saying, 'You have to meet her.'

'Your mother?' I gasp, sounding no doubt alarmed, as much as if he'd confessed to having stalked me for the past five years and only now in the grip of Nembutal had the courage to speak out and press the flesh and so forth. He wants me to meet his mother. Mercy!

'I have a mother,' he says quietly.

'And you want me to meet her?'

'She'll cope.'

'When?'

'Tomorrow?'

'And you really liked how I came across on TV?'

'Yes.'

'Enough to want me to meet your mother?'

'Yes.'

'Rabid?'

'That was the best part.'

I hop out of bed, pull on my Harlequins shirt. A souvenir of a gap-toothed out-half who left before dawn, I seem to recall, mystifyingly taking with him a black push-up inexpensive brassiere of mine. Anyway, now I'm having to cope with the searing wounds of my latest conquest.

'Did I say something?' he wants to know.

'You have to go,' I say and gather up and toss the bulk of his clothing at him. 'Because if I'm meeting your mother I can't feel compromised. Morally. Which I would do if you were to spend the night. So, please, if you wouldn't mind.'

'You're kidding?'

'Not in the least. You see, she'd know I slept with you, wouldn't she, and no matter that I may appear to you a sort of modern girl, with modern sensibilities and a grasp of all the usual practicalities, in fact I'm not, I'm terribly old-fashioned where mothers are concerned and meeting yours, I'm sure I'd only come out all blotches, weeping phobic blotches of guilt and trauma and psychosis. Yech!'

'But we already . . .'

'Trust me on this. I know mothers. Their powers of pinpointing moral frailty and blowing it all out of proportion.'

Finally, seeing the light, he gets out of bed, starts

dressing, muttering, swearing, as, outside, torrents of horizontal rain strike the side of the house.

He looks out of the window and turns to tell me, 'It's bucketing,' as if I should take pity on him and invite him back between my warm sheets.

'It's nothing,' I say, 'a touch of drizzle.'

At which point a terrific crack of thunder seems to shake the entire edifice, the very bricks and mortar, not to mention my mortal self. So much for my meteorological gifts. I bestow a dry little peck on his cheek as he leaves, then hop back into bed, pull the covers over my head, turn out the light.

I haven't seen a hair of him since. He calls of course. But I don't see much future there.

Jerry & Marie

I'd been buying bridal magazines for months and all of a sudden I thought what am I doing, this is some sort of sickness, some sort of pathological frenzy. There was a whole mountain of them stacked on the floor in my room. I took a long slow look at them and then all of a sudden I just spat at them, a small white gob of hot spit, which certainly took me by surprise as I'm hardly the spitting type. And instantly I scrabbled across the floor on my hands and knees to mop up the spit with the hem of my T-shirt. And I thought probably at that instant there was a man somewhere who'd pay a lot of money for me and my spit. I'd spit at him all night long for £1,000. And right away I berated myself for being weak. I told myself I must be stronger. I must be more Jerry Hall. I must be more Marie Helvin. Abiding. Pricier. Upmarket. No spitting for less than £10,000 and a Tiffany bracelet as per diem. Not to suggest that either Jerry Hall or Marie Helvin have ever spat for money in their lives. And then I think, they're both in their forties and I'm not halfway there yet so I don't really need to abide that much for a while more. Every dog must have its day. I can afford to make a few more mistakes. Get it out of my system. I have time on my side. When those two were my age they were probably making the same mistakes I'm making now. So, everything's going to be fine. I can make the same mistakes they did and work it all out when I'm older. Also, the mystique and elegance will no doubt come with the years. Does Marie Helvin have kids? Do you know who I'm talking about? If she doesn't, her dear friend Jerry has enough for both of them. In this modern age, so far as women are concerned, kids are no longer a prerequisite to any sort of lifetime fulfilment. This is one of my mother's fave tenets. However, there's a teensy flaw in my thinking. Unlike Jerry and Marie I am not a glamorous model with all the best physical accoutrements and alien allure . . . Jerry's from Texas and Marie's Hawaiian. A modest flutter of their exotic lashes and they're able to stun the entire gamut of native testosterone-dimmed nitwits. Whereas I'm from where? Basildon. Yes, Basildon. Who to blame for this tragic lapse in God's design? There must be someone to blame. It comes down to a choice between God and my mother. I blame my mother.

Jerry Corriente

Jerry Corriente has been coming to mind of late. A golfing Arizonan whom I met on holiday in Spain. He was thirty-something at the time. Thirteen, fourteen, fifteen years ago?

'What are you doing tomorrow?' he'd asked.

I'd replied, 'I'm sorry but I'm not interested in a relationship at this moment in time.'

'You can't help it, baby,' he'd said, grinning, or was it a leer, 'we're something, we have history.'

History? Maybe by American standards. Out on the course he'd noticed a flaw in my short game, introduced himself, suggested corrections. I'd ridden in on his buggy. Everything had been proper. His teeth shone out from his tanned face. We both appreciated how attractive he was. A bright diverting character. This genial conversation took place by the clubhouse pool, drinks in hand. My legs were painfully sunburned. His grandmother was a Quaid from Killaloe.

I said, 'I don't know you.'

'Yet,' he said.

'There's no future,' I said.

'I heard it all before,' he said.

'Not from me you haven't,' I said.

'You got me there,' he said, losing interest, starting to look around to see who else was there on display, available, and more amenable to his distinct charm.

That's all. Nothing happened. Nothing even transpired. I was saving myself at the time. Now I wish I'd saved him. Now he must be fifty, nicely weathered, comfortable. I look at myself and think, no, it wouldn't have washed.

Kenzo

I wake in the early morning to find him dressing so as to hurry home and change for the office. I admire his *Kenzo* black shoes and he tells me he bought them in Paris last August when the city was deserted and shopping was a pleasure. As he leans over to kiss me good morning I have to swallow my curiosity as to whom he visited Paris with. After he's gone I spend an agitated hour trying to get back to sleep but am unable to rid my mind of the realisation that no one visits Paris by themselves. It's just not done. Not even in August.

Lanzarote

I used to have this dream of living in Australia. Then it was Rio. Then it was San Francisco. Now it's Lanzarote. But life gets in the way. Life eats you up and shits you out. It's an entirely natural process.

Li

I had red, I guess you'd call it red, it was bright, really bright red hair, I was eighteen, this guy I was with was maybe late twenties, twenty-eight I think he said, he was a jockey, honestly, I remember I was looking at this wad of pink gum pressed on the bedboard over my head, glistening, all while he moved against me from behind, making me groan, like, I don't mean that he was making it happen for me, not a bit, I don't think he was my type, I don't think he was anyone's type, it was hard going, him working away, his forehead bumping against my neck, really icky drool from his mouth running down my back, he started biting at my shoulder, his teeth snagging on my bra straps, I mean I could have told him it wouldn't be a lot of fun but it was his idea to bum me and, since he was paying, I wasn't going to say, no, you know you're not really my type, or bumming turns me off, or there's other sweeter things you could do to me, but that's guys for you, they've got these strange ways of getting off, back then I don't think I thought about it that much, you know, it wasn't unusual, maybe there was something about me made guys want to bum me, anyway I tried to take my mind off what was happening, I said to him, I don't know, something like, won't you look at this wonderful homely decor, you just know it's made for beeping, he didn't know what I was on about, he went, what? and I was like not wanting to use a cruder term for what we were at, what he was at, I was saying, beeping per se is not a bad or demeaning act, of course like anything it really matters who's doing it to you, but basically it's just one more option looking to be covered (so long, of course, and this I don't say, so long as you're relaxed and lubed, really thoroughly lubed, then it needn't be, you know, an ordeal, not that I was ever, or ever wanted to be, a spokesperson for beeping), and then it hit him, he said, you're not from around here, which as it happens he was wrong, I was, born and bred I said, my daddy's a dairy farmer, Friesians mostly, my mother keeps geese and writes poetry, and I could see he was forming this picture in his head, keeping him hard, you know, wanting to know, wondering whether there were more like me at home, depends where you look I told him, God, you know, some people, now I think of it, doing him really was a pain, I just kept yacking away, probably, I suppose, to try and keep my mind off what in actual fact he was doing to me, you

know, back there, I'm supposed to be flighty, I told
him, like my mother's sister Becky, she's a dental
hygienist, and I had to laugh because I don't know about
Becky, my aunt, I never asked her, but right then flighty
was getting me bummed, then with a God, from him,
and an I bet, and an oh my, from me, he was done,
grunting one last foamy breath in my ear and we were
just lying there, a phone ringing somewhere down the
hall, he rolled away from me, stared at the ceiling, I got
my gum back, peeled it off the bedboard, popped it
back in my mouth, rolled over to face him, what's your
name, he asked, Li, I said, it's Dutch for truth, and
when he said nothing I asked him if he had any Dutch
friends, but he just shook his head, showed no interest
whatsoever and I said, of course I'm not really Dutch,
I'm Irish, you know, though there are loads of Dutch
people living round here, Germans even, English,
strange, he only nodded, then I told him he had a nice
body and he said he broke it often enough and I
remember reaching out to run a finger on his teeth,
your teeth, I said, and he was sensitive about them, you
could tell from the way he moved his head away from
me and clamped his lips shut, which only made me go
after him, lean up close, look right in his face until he
mumbled, I know, and I said, I like them, they're kind
of, something, too big maybe, something not exactly
wrong, something, too big for your head maybe, I
tickled him until he smiled at me, showed a flash of

teeth, and he asked me where we were and I told him the name of the town and he asked me was it my place and I said, are you kidding, don't you recognise a swish hotel when you take a ride in one and he laughed and I picked the TV zapper off the night table and turned on the TV with the sound off and tossed the zapper on a chair and ignored the TV and asked him how old he was, twenty-eight, or maybe he said he was twenty-nine, something like that anyway, less than thirty, and then after a while he said, I don't remember how we got here, and I told him he drove, which amazed him, so I explained how I gave directions and helped him with the steering, which somehow reminded me of the smart comments and sly remarks my father used to mutter about women, sneering at how little they were good for, how much they were crap at, forming opinions, having a sense of direction, this before my sisters and I got together and put him straight on certain issues, aspects of gender, offensive posturing, babbling chauvinism, there are five of us and we definitely changed his outlook, stupid eejit thick bastard, the jockey and I had a laugh at that, he was happy to see my side of things and grateful I'd got him here in one piece, more or less, and he took my hand and ran it all over his body, I broke every bone in my body, he said, one time or another, and you're only twenty-eight, I said, and damn proud of your bones, you'd better believe it, he said and I said, what about your heart, and kissed his skinny flat chest and he nipped at my nose and his hands roamed over the bony side of my hips, then he said, you have high hips, and I said, high hips, no tits, and from the way he looked at me I could tell I was constantly surprising him, he looked at me and smiled, I don't know, he threw his legs over the side of the bed and I saw he still had his socks on and he rubbed a hand to his face, lifted his jeans from off the floor and pulled them on, then he fished out a pill bottle, went to the sink, popped a pill, washed it down with a handful of water, went to the window and looked outside, and without looking at me he said, I've never been down this way before, what's it like, so I told him, this is the best part, and he turned to look at me and I stretched out, luxuriating on the bed but he didn't come over, he pulled on his T-shirt and looked around for his boots, see these boots, he said, when I was in the States I drove eight hundred miles to buy these boots, seven-hundred-buck Tony Barja's or Lama's, I don't remember which he said, it was something like Larja's or Bama's, your hat's in the car, I reminded him, he stood up then, and you could see he was feeling uncomfortable, that was always an awkward time, he was anxious to be off, I asked him for a tissue and he threw me this towel from the sink and I wiped myself and then I leaned over the edge of the bed, my head hanging upside down, my hair all over the place as I searched around on the floor and under the bed for my things and pulled my dress towards me, a little green cotton print, like what they call a tea dress, and gave it a shake but they weren't there so I tossed away the dress and picked up my tights, hot-pink knit ones, you know, bright, ribbed, some guys have a thing about, a fetish, and took a quick look in them, then I leaned up on an elbow and craned my neck and looked around the room without seeing what I was looking for, so I sat up altogether and watched him watching me wiggle into those tights, then he caught my eye and gave a little bashful wave and slipped outside, and I hopped out of bed and went to the door to slide the safety bolt, instead of a chain it was one of those kind of a hinged bolt would let the door open just a crack but if you pushed at it expecting it to open and the hinged bolt held then it made a terrific snapping noise, and sure enough a moment later there's a knocking on the door and it opened a crack, snagging loudly on the safety catch and I pulled on my leather jacket and hurried to release the catch and let him back in and he just grabbed me by the shoulders and pushed me down until he could stick his tongue in my mouth and kissed me until I was about to gag and he said, I came back to say good night, and I said, it's two-o-fucking-clock and anyway you're not supposed to kiss me, and then I kissed him to show there were no hard feelings and pushed him out the door again, a hand on his butt and fixed the bolt once more and threw off the jacket, picked my dress off the floor and slipped it on and right while I was doing it up, you'd know it, the door crashed open once more, and there's the same loud crack as it jammed on the bolt so I walked over again and released the bolt and let him back in and told him, you don't have to worry about me, I'm fine, I've been kicked worse than this milking a damn cow, and he said, that's a nice dress, and I said, you like it, it cost me four pounds at the Salvation Army, and I pushed him out the door one more time, went through the same old deal with the deadbolt, only this time I waited by the door and sure enough the bolt snapped loud a third time and I couldn't help smiling as I let him back in, he wanted to know had I a number he could call in a day or two so we could meet up, I shook my head, explained, I'm flying to London for a week, please, he said and I thought what can you do, and he smiled at me this crooked smile and I looked around for something to write my number on, asked him have you got a pen but he didn't so I went around opening up all these drawers until I found paper, but no pen, then I remembered, and got a lipstick from my jacket and wrote a number on his T-shirt, then, and I don't think either of us could have expected something like this to happen, there was this knock on the door and we just looked at each other wondering who it could be and I walked over and opened the door to find this peed-off woman, old, you know, like forty, dowdy, scowling at me, might have been Mathias's mother, Mathias's boss, though she hadn't hardly an accent, but, you know, snooty, I just couldn't place her, who she was, what she wanted, she was right at it, yack yack in my face, spit flying, I could hear you all the way down the hall in the office, maybe you'd like to consider other people and quieten it down a bit, and just to wind her up I asked, is the television too loud, and I mean the television was playing all right but the sound was like totally off, and she went, you know very well what I'm talking about, Miss, and she started to like glare in this really old-fashioned hostile way at my friend, you know, the jockey, who I swear to God was actually blushing at this point, and I went, what, in this wide-eyed clueless way, you know, and the woman pointed at the bolt on the door and I said, vaguely, that was only once, and the woman wagged her stubby fingers and held up four right in my face, you know, meaning four times, which it wasn't, and she said, no more, you hear me, and I only shrugged as she left, but this time when I shut the door I didn't set the bolt and the jockey was standing there looking at me and looking at his precious boots and I went all glum and said, I'm hopeless at this, and started sniffling about the bloody cow from hormone hell and then I realised like, my friend, the jockey, he wasn't paying me any attention whatsoever, he was all wrapped up studying the bed pillows, you know, climbing on there to stick his face right up close until he turned around all triumphant with a thirty-inch strand of red hair, one of mine, in his hand and I told him he could keep it, I said, it's all yours, and he showed his teeth and wound the hair round his fingers and I said, no extra charge, and grabbed him by the collar and bundled him out the door and feeling sort of woozy and drained, you know, I just sat on the edge of the bed and pulled my doodahs from inside one of my DMs, which is where I finally remembered I'd shoved them, orange high-cut nothings, brighter than my hair, damn, you know when you find you're half-dressed and worse, got everything on in the wrong order, arsebackways, thinking all I've got to do, I've got to dress myself all over, so I get my tights pulled halfway down before I think life really is too short to worry about details like that and I stuffed the pants in my jacket pocket, forced my feet into the DMs and tied them loosely, took one last look round the room, picked up my jacket, checked that my passport, plane ticket, lipstick, johnnies, the tiny tub of jelly and all of eighty pounds were in the pocket then I bent to check myself in a mirror and pushed my hands through my hair, found the room key and walked out the door without closing it or turning off the TV, I don't know, maybe I was hungry or tired but I felt sort of faint walking along the hotel corridor, and I bumped against the walls a couple of times but really by the time I got downstairs I was feeling fine, I just tossed the key at Mathias who had his face in a crumpled old wanker's tabloid all the while picking glop from his scalp, looking a bit wormy tonight, Mathias, I said and he looked confused at me as I went out the door, he was verminous I'm sure, I can't imagine what I'd have done if he'd like ever wanted to date me, it wasn't much of a stretch to reach where I wanted to get and then the next thing you know a car comes from nowhere and slows and I walk over and the driver rolls down the window and we speak and he drives off and I go lean against a shopfront, shove my hands deep in my jacket pockets, blow gum until another car approaches and pretty much the same routine, you know, walk to the kerb when the car slows and stops, the motor keeps running, this time I take the gum from my mouth and hold it behind my back because sometimes gum puts people off, and he's nervous, a little unsure and possibly guilty and I try to put him at his ease and smile while I'm speaking to him and it's on and I walk slowly round the front of the car and pat the gum on the roof before getting in the passenger seat and he drives me away and I ask him his name and he asks me mine and I catch him looking at my legs, and I think, you know, about things, different things, about art, about Picasso, about remembering to rinse my contact lenses, about London, about Mathias and his mother or manager or whoever she was, about how I look in my old boots and my green dress and my black jacket, about cutting my hair, changing the colour, dozens and hundreds and thousands of thoughts, all of them taking time, using up my life, and what can you do, you know, only think them

Li's Mask

I used to rub backs for a living. Now I rob banks. Hence the mask. I like that word. Hence.

Li's Philosophy

You tell men what they like to hear, you own them . . . body, heart and soul. Not forgetting their wallets.

Life

You could summarise my life like this. I was born. I grew tits. I got fucked a lot of times. I married. I broke up. I got fucked some more times. I'm here now. I don't know a lot about what lies ahead for me. No one likes to think that things won't change, you know, for the better.

List

Mosquito repellent. Chunky KitKat. Anything Clinique to remind him of me. Creatine to remind me of him. Brillo. Muji chopsticks. Pregnancy tester kit outfit thingy indicator strip turns blue when you wee while knocked-up, every girl should have one. A colour postcard featuring a generic view of central London, BT Tower, Centre Point. Toblerone maybe. Big Toblerone. Nobuyoshi Araki. How to become a Japanese pornographer and the minor surgery which that would entail. Paris. Salamanca. Jamie Oliver. Clogs. Tocca. Tokyo. *Vogue*. Babington House, Somerset. Do not go down on men you've known less than thirty-six hours. Amazon.com. On the other hand. Shave. Strive against becoming Ellie type of girl, big hair, big teeth, terribly *joie de vivre*, shag-happy, always ready with the after-dinner contraceptive, wouldn't know who Eric Cantona was if he up and bit her on the fanny. Russell & Bromley painted snake sandals. Jarvis Adams. All of my other foibles. Cider. Chinese, Indian, Greek. Try Russian on Mike like he wanted. More of that sort of grand optimism. Much more. Kleenex Double Velvet. Asleep in each other's arms, i.e. Jaap Boddeke. Goldy leafy stripy strappy top from Oasis. Simon wanking. I may have a disease. He's a clot, they're all clots, my life is clotted with clots, I am the queen of clots. Price new

Motorola cellphone. The same dream of Wendi Deng, Rupert and I, call it a nightmare. Blood everywhere. Lycra. Cadbury's Snack Shortcake six-pack. Cellular telephones with vibrapowerpack. Electric toothbrush ditto. Ray Parlour. David Batty. Clara's tits. Jonny Lee Miller. He tongued me. Dizzy trollops in a loo. Young. Bioré strips. Bioré burn. Hormones. Chocolate. Crisps. Lousy air quality. Bicycling. Winter makes you fat. Tofu. Bellyache. My failure to religiously cleanse and tone like my mother advised and forewarned. Always wee before sex. Ideas for money-making websites. Ideas.com. Memories.com. Feelings.com. Marriage .com. Truelove.com. Find-a-Husband.com. Nuns-in-Bondage.com. ChangeDealers.com. Exercise.com. Shop.com. Stopit.com! Refresh list. Check out organically dyed cerise cotton Habitat sheets. Research Jordan trip. May. Lily's birthday. Eddie's party. Reschedule Dr Schnabel. Pedicure. Stock up on sherry, E, blow. Shoes. Squander savings. Try for BBC job else ask old shop job back. Try New Bond Street. Talk to Casper Gehry. Royal Free Hospital outpatients. The cavalry officer with the shaved neck. Stephen what? Watt? Witter? Visa bill. Lipgloss. Eyeliner. Tampons. Making a mess in someone's Saab. Leather upholstery. Making a mess on someone's Merc. That racing-car driver bird-dogging me in Milan. Massimo shampooing me. Getting my tongue back, thank you very much. Uniball eye pen.

iBooks everywhere. Reeboks. Discount from Dee Dee at the Gap. Walk down Long Acre, keeping an eye out for essentials, bargains, perfect love, that sort of thing.

Lost

I remember leaving the coffee shop around lunchtime and going down the street to pick up some vodka and gin at the off-licence. Then turning left through the archway, along the alley, past a group of schoolboys eating chips and sneering at passing girls, who went quiet when they saw me, waited for me to pass before resuming their taunting of the girls. On past the pub and into the car park. I couldn't remember where I'd left the car so I walked back and forth along the lines of parked cars until ages later I found it. I don't think anyone was watching me, noticing my strange behaviour. I put the bottles on the back seat. I sat in wearily behind the wheel and tilted the rear-view mirror to check my lipstick. It was fine. I fingered my skirt away from my knees, back into the fork of my thighs, and reversed out of there, my chin on my left shoulder, stopped, spun the power-steered wheel, faced forward into the sun, shifted gear, fingered my sunglasses from the door side pocket, the engine humming, clutch buried underfoot, stationary, sitting there, hesitant, for all the world like a woman with no idea where she was going.

Lovers

Mum is distracted. She doesn't like it now that I've begun to call her Hilary to her face.

'It makes me sound so tired,' she says.

'Your friends call you Hilary,' I say.

'What friends?' she says.

'You have friends,' I say.

'Lovers,' she says.

And she makes it sound so sad. Like it's all just become an unbearable burden.

Loving Jude

His name is Jude, he works with my mother, and I know that he's gay. Right from the start, the first time I see him, I know that he's gay. Everyone knows that he's gay. This doesn't stop me falling for him. I follow him everywhere, probably making his life a misery. I wear my school uniform as if I'm about to step out of it with a single shrug and drape myself over him like a bright white mink. I'm gorgeous but it makes no difference to him. He's very nice to me, patient and polite. He never tells me to shoo. He never mocks me. The longer it goes on the more convinced I am that he's the one for me. He can't appreciate how won over I am by him, by every last inchy bit of him.

'You must be Esther,' he says the first time we meet.

'Ess,' I say, and he doesn't hear, he thinks I've said yes and he smiles and leans close and I say it again, 'Ess,' and his teeth are so white and his skin so clear and his bones so fine and his scent so clean and understated, I'm feeling faint, my heart thundering, my breath a whisper, and as a joke, to show his amusement, his ear comes towards my lips and I say it a third time, tip it softly in his waiting ear, 'My name is Ess.'

Jude's a magazine writer and I collect everything he writes and construct a little grotto of his work and then I get one of our housekeeper Mae's holy relics and rub it between thumb and forefinger so that he'll love me and we'll go off together somewhere and live happy ever after.

One time my mother comes in my room while I'm reading and I flick over the magazine so she can't see I've been mooning over Jude, sniffing the page, licking it, and she sits on the edge of the bed and picks up the magazine and opens it to Jude's faintly moist picture and tells me, 'Ess, darling, you know that he's gay, don't you?' And I shrug my indifference, though right then I'm not at all sure what gay is and is not, the ins and outs of it, as it were, I mean, I'm fourteen, and it seems to me whatever else it is, it can't be terminal.

I spend days hanging around trying to get through to him. He tells me straight out he doesn't like girls. I tell him I'm not like other girls. He says, 'I can see that.' I take this as an encouraging sign and move my arms closer, vainly hoping to enhance my scant bosoms and convert him.

'Ess,' he says. 'Forget it.'

'You don't fool me,' I say.

'Trust me,' he says, 'I could not be fooling you less.'

'Helen tells me never to trust boys.'

'Your mother's right,' he says, 'you mustn't ever.'

'You love Helen, don't you?'

'No.'

'I'm not a virgin if that's what's worrying you.'

'Girls don't do it for me, Ess.'

'We could be happy together.'

'You're too young to be thinking about being together with anyone.'

'How do I know until I try.'

'Try?'

'I want to try you.'

'I don't excite you and you don't ditto.'

'What's ditto? I'll try ditto if that's what you like.'

'You don't have ditto to start with, sweetie.'

'Sex isn't everything. I can get a million boys to have sex with.'

I persevere. He tells me not to be desperate. I tell him I'm not desperate, I just chose him.

One day at his place:

Me: 'I have to talk to you.'

Him: 'And I have to go to work.'

Me: 'Let me wait here for you. Please.'

Him: 'I don't know when I'll be back.'

Me: 'I don't mind.'

Him: 'Ess.'

Me: 'I love you.'

Him: 'I have to go now. I have to do this interview. You can stay for a while. OK?'

After he leaves, I go through every last item in his possession. I press my face in his clothes. I brush my teeth with his toothbrush. I shave my legs with his razor. I slather on his moisturiser. I finesse already invisible brows with his tweezers. I lie on his bed and wrap the sheets around me. Then I take out the bottle of pills I lifted from Helen's cabinet and set them all out in a long straight line on his night table. I bring a carton of milk from the fridge and pour some in a glass. It all looks very wholesome. I start on the pills. Swallowing. Washing down with milk. I pick up the phone and set it on the bed where I can reach it. I chew some more pills. I pop a can of Pringles and start eating them, leaving tiny tasty crumbs on the duvet. I stretch out on the bed and make the call.

'You know why I picked you, don't you,' I say. 'Because I knew I'd never be just another piece of pussy to you. You didn't even have to fuck me, you know.'

When he finds me, I'm on the floor in his bathroom. He hurries to my side like he's supposed to and kneels and lifts my head onto his lap and pushes my hair from my soiled face. I smile wanly like I've practised. 'I'm fat,' I say. I say, 'God, I'm so sorry.' Weeping and whispering, 'I'm fat and I'm ugly. Too fat and too ugly for you to want to love me.'

He gets down on the floor alongside me and pulls me into his arms. Which is when my nerve fails me. I notice my vomit is rubbing off on his hands and his clothes. 'What a pig I am,' I say, and try to pull away but he holds on tight to me and I struggle and he clings to me as I jerk and inch my way across the floor, bringing him with me. Finally, I stop, exhausted, and he lies across me, his face in my hair, moaning my name, his hand moving up under my shirt, searching for my breast.

Of course, it all comes to nothing. But at least it doesn't end badly because later through Jude I meet the great (Franz) Frendt, and he photographs me and after that I sign with an agency and change my name and the rest is history.

Macey

I was sleeping with that crazy Macey when the phone
went hysterical and we both of us jumped out of bed
and fought each other to cut it off. If you want to know
the truth, Macey is not all that wonderful. She has
luscious skin and beautiful breasts but no sense of dress
or occasion or what you'd call decorum.

I met her when I went in this hardware store on
Gallatin and 9th. You know the kind of place: small,
dusty, with an out-of-control stock and prices from the
eighties. She was looking for a cold-chisel, if you can
believe that. I forgot, she also has this glorious voice to
go with her skin and her breasts; and her family, her
mother in particular, had all this money and property
for ever so long and that kind of had an effect on the
type of person she was. She was interested crucially in
her own personality and focused in such a way that left
her absolutely lacking in compassion. That's what I say.
Anyhow, you don't have to take my word for it.

Well, she had some disagreement with the store-
keeper and for the heck of it I took her side and the guy
was fairly aggrieved and decided he wanted us out of
there right away and he made the most dreadful mistake
of taking her by the arm. Well, Macey just went head-
over-heels ballistic, pummeling the poor chump with
her dainty fine fists until she had him backed into a
corner and just as she was reaching for this hoe with a

hickory handle I intervened and said not to bother and she didn't.

The handle was hickory because I went back later and bought it in an attempt to mollify Mr Willnecker who was not without friends in the Chamber of Commerce and he said it was hickory and charged me hickory prices.

Well, anyway, we got out of there and she seemed fiery, which grabs me, and I suggested we get ourselves a coffee or something and she nodded her head and we went down the street along Gallatin and crossed over town via Main toward the railway where you could get breakfast twenty-four hours and as we went along she pointed out her car, a cherry-red Camaro, and right then I couldn't fit that in with the rest of her. She didn't seem at all girly to me.

In the heel of the hunt she discovered a cracked fingernail which I said I could fix in a jiffy and that's how we got together back at my place where I offer a wide range of beauty treatments − I call it *La Dolce Femme* − with the blinds drawn. But it doesn't explain the phone calls we've been getting all hours. The only thing to do is shut up shop, get out in the country in the Camaro and see what the world's made of.

Even if I don't play my cards right I'm starting to figure the least she can do when it's time for her to move on is leave the keys with me. I'd even drive her to the airport and squeeze her and kiss her and wave her adieu, you know, and throw in a full body wax, gratis. I would. Cross my heart and hope to fry.

Mal de Mer

later I requested a teaspoon of bread soda in a glass of warm water to combat my heartburn after which I slept tolerably well and in the morning we paid our fare and walked carrying our bags as far as the Gare something or other whence we took the bus to Bourg sur Gironde on the trail of some transplanted Roman friend his friend more than mine Lucilla Marchetti in the course of the journey I experienced not for the first time since leaving Barcelona awful excruciating rectal spasms which I presumed to be some way connected to a haemor-rhoidal condition it is disheartening to walk into a book-store and read in a home medical reference book that the condition is irreversible one of the accumulative infirmities attendant with ageing I am twenty-two and my beau tells me I am deliciously configured I know what he means I have my own hair eyes teeth breasts thighs my hearing is good my bones sound my visceral parts uncomplaining that is until these recent spasms I am not constipated my diet is healthy regular fresh in Bourg sur Gironde we got off the bus and walked in the hot sun two or three dusty miles and Lucilla wasn't home but her friend Mirabelle was Mirabelle walked in small mincing steps and would bizarrely only speak to us in unremarkable English I decided on the spot she was certainly promiscuous though this was probably simple-minded on my part she offered us cheese and coffee and told us there was no alcohol in the house though we hadn't mentioned alcohol while we sat at the kitchen table she told us she was going outside to lie in the sun and smiled I thought because we were flushed and sun-surfeited from our journey after we'd finished the cheese I went to look around the house while my beau went outside I watched from a window as he approached Mirabelle who'd removed her shirt and skirt and lay alongside them on the brown dead grass in her plain underclothes which showed off her tan while I watched my beau sit beside her and force her into small-talk I realised this whole trip had been a mistake whatever had spurred us out of the hot fly-plagued city now seemed vague and tenuous idle even then Lucilla came in the house and greeted me holding my shoulders kissing me she told me I had lost weight she told me my beau was worried about me I told her I'd just been out of sorts that there was nothing the matter with me a good beating wouldn't fix she didn't see the humour I began to feel shaky in a flash I understood how everything was up for grabs Lucilla took my hand and sat me down I tried to explain how everything bobbled so I couldn't fix on anything she didn't know the word bobble and as I sought a Spanish or Italian equivalent I realised I could never share my grief with anyone I was flushed and Lucilla had tears in her eyes as she embraced me again and held me tight and didn't let go until I felt the grief wane I wanted to tell her the grief is waning the grief is waning but desperately wanted to avoid reminding myself of nothing more than a terrible third-rate actress Lucilla handed me a tissue and I blew my nose while she blew hers then she slapped her hands down on her bare thighs and laughed as they stung and reddened she stood up and trailed a hand through my hair I asked her what there was to do and she told me there were a couple of cafés she liked in Bourg sur Gironde or we could fly a kite I lay back then while she went to wash her hands and face and brush out her hair and I thought of flying a blue kite lost against blue sky stumbling over the parched hillside Lucilla came back and began to explain the workings of their temperamental shower Mirabelle wandered in and perched on the back of the sofa I resolved to do something memorable something that would reduce everything to wrappable transportable graspable essentials something inexcusable abrasive bad why in order to spite everyone and rid myself of all this whispering and tippy-toeing concern and blaagh and then what then who will be left to chide me haemorrhoids I suppose I picked through my T-shirt adjusting the straps and cups of my brassiere one more time I might as well have been picking my nose the way Mirabelle looked at me my beau came in I announced I thought I'd try the shower I thought everyone looked at me as if I were a true unfortunate but how could they know I began humming I would never be distracted again I went in the shower room and undressed and called for Lucilla and she came and set the water for me I waited until she was gone and the steam gathered before I cut open my veins with the blade of a carpet knife I'd brought from Barcelona the hospital was horrid I spent weeks longing to be gay and vivid then I went home to my beau sensibly or so I thought at the time

Manolos

Today I'm going to wear Manolos, a grey woollen skirt, a pink cashmere sweater, a creamy Prada overcoat. In total, a lot of money. And you thought I was some kind of streetwalking sex worker on the breadline.

Meeting Mrs K

On my way home from work I popped across to the Danish place for a croissant and thought about stealing a magazine from the stand outside the tube station but as I was feeling chipper I paid up and smiled and said cheerio to the fat man. It's a thin line, isn't it, between here and there, life and death, truth and dare. Love ever after is not one of my concerns. My mother wonders what will happen when life finally dawns on me. I say, Mother, stop being a holy cow. She shakes her head in scornful disbelief. She wants me to be real. She wants me married. She wants me to be true to myself. I say, cunt to that. She says she doesn't believe it when I'm being like this. She expects everything to be authentic. That's high. She was always high. There is no remedy for high. Then halfway home I ran into someone, a faintly familiar face which spoke to me.

'Sylvia Glade,' it said.

And I said, 'How do, Mrs Khan?'

And she said, 'Very well, thank you. And you?'

And I said, 'Ditto.'

And she said, 'Your lovely sisters?'

And I said, 'All married, I'm afraid.'

And she said, 'And you?'

And I said, 'I'd rather shoot myself.'

Maybe I alarmed her a little with my vehement stance but all the same she nodded approvingly and went on her way. A long time ago, the lady's son, her youngest son, Yumnah, Yumnah Khan, nice boy, wrote me a poem when I was twelve and he fifteen about my pellucid pelt. I had to look it up, what it meant, pellucid. First rule, if there has to be rules, and of course there doesn't, always come as you are. And go. I do. My mother is always disappointed when life lets her down. She always hopes life is going to be clever and elegant like some Cary Grant effortless light comedy and then when it's shite and misery she takes to her bed and moans about reality and authenticity and facing up to and accepting the real world. All the same it's nice when someone calls you pellucid even though you know it's all a crock of shit. Especially then.

Meeting Tobe

Out of the blue I get this phone call from my mother. She tells me something which she claims she'd have preferred to tell me face-to-face but it just can't wait. She's getting married again. Once I catch my breath I try to sound interested and pleased for her. I even remember to ask who the lucky fellow is. His name's Tobe with an E but a silent one . . . like Toblerone without the lerone. He's a model. And they're trying for a baby. At forty-nine? I don't like to ask. And how old is Tobe? Likewise . . . aspects of lurking chronic nausea keep me from enquiring.

So, naturally, in the wake of all these good tidings I catch a train to Manchester right away. I call her from the train telling her to do nothing drastic until I get there. Can only hope and trust she's had some sort of brainstorm that will have faded and passed by the time I reach her. Have forgotten all own personal woes in rush and surprise. What if own mother and self produce sprogs within hours of one another? What do they put in these cheese sandwiches? And where do they still find white bread of such glutinous texture it must take fourteen-plus days to digest?

Reach mother's house in wretched state. Tobe opens door. Age: thirties. Appearance: tan, as in leather; buff enough; black tight CK T a size too small to show off ripply washboard abs; Roadrunner tattoo on exposed bulky right pectoral; low-slung khaki cargoes; blue foamy flip-flops; neatly pedicured toes; pierced eyebrow; redolent of salon 2-in-1 shampoo and conditioner.

'Heather,' he exclaims, grabbing me for a hug and a peck on both cheeks, like we're long-lost bosom buddies, which clinch provides me with irrefutable proof he's got better tits than me.

I go, 'Tobe?' And right away he goes, 'I've got some bad news, I'm afraid Hilary's in the hospital.' And I go, 'Hilary?'

And he goes, 'Your mum.'

And I go, 'I know my mum. What happened?'

And he goes, 'She fell.'

And I go, 'Mum fell?'

And he goes, 'Hilary, yes, downstairs.'

And I go, 'Oh . . . my . . . God.'

And he goes, 'But she's going to be fine.'

And I go, 'She fell downstairs?'

And he goes, 'Yes.'

And I go, 'Where?'

And he goes, 'No, she fell down the stairs.'

And I go, 'Fell down the stairs?'

And he goes, 'Yes.'

And I go, 'Why?'

And he goes back at me, 'Why?'

And I go, 'Yes, why?'

And he goes, 'What sort of a question is why?'

And I go, suspiciously now, 'Did you . . .?'

And he goes, 'I beg your pardon,' sounding all aghast and clapping his hands to his ears with what strikes me as a fairy pose of incredulity. Trust my mother to have misread the true nature of Tobe.

'I'm sorry,' I go, ashamed of myself.

And he goes, 'My God, but you're even more paranoid than Hilary said.'

And I go, 'Paranoid's a big word.'

And he goes, 'OK, you have to hear it from someone, it may as well be me.'

And I go, 'You pushed her?'

And he goes, 'She jumped.'

And I go, 'She?'

And he goes, 'She was upset.'

And I go, 'My mother upset?'

And he goes, 'She just . . .'

And I go, 'Jumped?'

And he goes, 'Yes, she . . .'

And I go, 'Jumped?'

And he goes, 'Yes.'

And I go, 'Oh, my, God.'

And he goes, 'She's going to be fine.'

And I go, 'Stop saying that.'

And he goes, 'But she is.'

And I go, 'She's, I don't understand, why did she?'

And he goes, 'Jump?'

And I go, 'Yes.'

And he goes, 'I, we, she somehow got the impression she and I were about to embark on, what would have been for me, a novel endeavour.'

And I go, 'You asked her to marry you?'

And he goes, 'No, see, but, yes, that's possibly where the initial misunderstanding may have arisen.'

And I go, 'You didn't ask her to marry you?'

And he goes, 'Of course not.'

And I go, 'And she didn't propose to you?'

And he goes, 'I'm not the marrying type.'

And I go, 'You're gay?'

And he goes, 'Bless my soul, whatever gave you that idea?'

And I go, 'Averse to marriage. I don't know.'

And he goes, 'No, I, it's simply I have other plans.'

And I go, 'Another floozy?'

And he goes, 'Your mother's not a . . .'

And I jump in, going, 'That's not what I said, I never said she was anything.'

And he goes, 'Will you relax.'

And I go, 'Where is she? I have to see her.'

And he goes, 'Heather.'

And I say, 'What?'

And I think for an instant, gay or not, he's about to hit on me, and I shake my head and move to the door and wait for him to fulfil whatever fleeting role he has in the story of my life.

'Let me get my keys,' he says, 'and I'll drive you to the hospital.'

'That would be nice,' I say.

Only then do I notice he has this wonderfully spun, tight little bum.

Poor Mum. Has a cracked tibia. Tobe doesn't care to come in. Drops me and runs. Leaves me to explain to Mum how he's packing his things, clearing out, moving to Bradford, which I suspect may not be the full truth. All for the best, whatever party town he's really headed for.

But Mum when I tell her doesn't agree.

She goes, 'The baby?'

So I go, 'What baby?'

And she goes, 'My baby?'

And I go, 'Mother, look at me, I'm no longer a . . .'

And she goes, 'Heather, I'm talking about Tobe and I striving for a little bundle of . . .' and she breaks off, sobbing.

'Oh, Mum,' I go, and take her in my arms and let her cry away.

Later, I'm drained and crawl up onto Mum's hospital bed and fall asleep. And later still, I wake to hear her chatting up the weary-looking, though still attractive, young doctor who comes to eyeball her, hopefully rid her of delusions re her mobility plus any reprise of motherhood and all its attendant perils. Long after visiting hours have finished I'm shooed away and assured she's in good hands for the next week or so. My conscience clear, I leave the hospital, find a taxi and just make the last train down south.

Miscarry

What comes out is me miscarrying. Blood and bits of tissue over the course of a day. They take me to the hospital and leave me two days there. I don't care what they do to me. I don't care what happens to me. I look at the nurses and don't see what they see. I look at the doctors and find they're men the same as the rest of them only dressed up in white and smelling clean like they're the angels of mercy we all cry out for. They ask me whose the baby is. I shake my head. They ask me who's the father. I bite my tongue until I taste blood. They ask me don't I know I'm underage. I start to weep. They name names. It wasn't like that, I say, it wasn't like that at all.

Mr Glanton

Going into and about town. Veiled or masked if I could. Heavy liquid foundation laid on to conceal the blow's yellowing sequela. Sunglasses. Hair unbound in a veil effort. The solicitor Mr Glanton's office on Market Street. I outline my intention to seek a change of scenery, vacate the house, the neighbourhood; and engage him to look after whatever matters should arise in my absence.

'How long do you plan on being away?' he asks.

'Indefinitely,' I say. 'I'll let you know where I am as soon as I get settled.'

'Honor.'

'Yes?'

'Don't stay away from us for too long this time, will you?'

I find him looking at my legs . . . despite the high split of the flannel jersey skirt there's no wilful infringement of decorum on my part . . . my stockinged legs laid sideways at an angle and pressed together. My shapely legs. I try to remember, did I ever flirt with him. Certainly there's no recollection of his ever having pursued me. Only a nagging open-sided caveat — I'm finding that I was never any better than I had to be where morals and habit were concerned. Now I smile at Mr Glanton — a married man to my best recollection — and rise to my feet. He comes from behind his desk and takes my arm and walks me to the door and I go down the stairs by myself, conscious of him watching me, the black Mizrahi suit, the problematic heels on the shallow steps, a sideways step at a time, my bearing disdainful, bored.

Monkey

I'm going through the listings trying to find my bearings between Covent Garden, garage, jungle, drum'n'bass, house, techno, trance. I'm supposed to be searching for something for us to do at the weekend. A proper dating activity. But all he knows is football, and Fraser, if pushed, admits to being a Spurs supporter and I just don't get that, any of it. So if it's a choice between White Hart Lane and, say, Highbury, I always opt for London Zoo.

And here we are, lying on the grass in the park, having spent a couple of hours drifting round the cages. The smell and the animal cries still reaching us. His fingers playing lightly with the buttons on my shirt, lifting the white cotton for a peek at my lacy cups joined by a tiny white bow which seems wondrous to him. I close my eyes, moan comfortably.

'Take me,' I say.

'Take you where?'

'Take me.'

He finally gets it and laughs self-consciously. I always thought blokes dreamed of girls saying things like that to them. But Fraser's behaving like he's threatened by my being so forthright. Or maybe he's just darkly amused by my foibles?

'What's so funny?' I say.

'Take me?' he says.

'Don't you want to?'

At last he grasps that maybe I'm serious and takes a long slow look around. There are people in the park. Strangers. Equipped with eyes and ears and sniffy dogs.

'Here?' he says. 'Now?'

I smile my assent, shield my eyes against the sun.

'Not in front of the monkeys?' he wants to know.

I leave him no choice and finally he leans over me, gives me some tongue, reaches for a hard-to-pin-down nipple, awkwardly inserts his hand and prods my breast blindly, uncomfortably, not getting us very far. I'm wishing he were more forceful, less twiddly, when suddenly he pops up, alarmed, skittish, like one of those prairie-dog sentries, checking to see whether he's being observed. I pull him back down, urging him to molest me, arching my back, turning my breast against his palm. He gains in aptitude. And somewhere beyond wire fencing and high shrubbery, the monkeys grow violently agitated.

Myriem

bitter to the end though the morphine is beginning to make me of all things candid the nurses here are invariably handsome well-paid dour and tan I remember the hours spent in the old garden and the wonderful sensation of having my dress billow and gust against my face and Maman holding my little hand to slap it so hard attempting through barely comprehensible cruelty to try and make me more modest I was never amenable I would be compelled to play a duet on the piano made in Japan mid-sixties with my obnoxious cousin Ginger-breath whom I would tease and pinch with regular impunity to this day she is a cheerful cretin sending me handwritten notes suggesting she hopes I am feeling better or will soon be doing so and then numbingly reporting on the state of her current pregnancy or her husband's sprint through middle management I was a Leninist at first naturally enough and later a willing Trotskyite but never ever a Maoist or Stalinist when I was eight I could leap into the sea and swim around Uncle's yacht twenty times without flagging I was Uncle's pest I didn't care he was seventy then and incontinent and only left his bed for his wheelchair to be strolled around the deck by some vain Italian or Greek crewman it was quite the spectacle and I never made a hand of stomaching it the nurses can be stroppy at times either because of my nature or what my sickness is Maman directs them how they must turn me every two hours and rub in the creams that prevent bedsores but Maman is never around she faxes them I ask them to bring me my lyre and when they refuse I bribe one of them with the promise of two thousand French francs to fax my mother my desire to be reunited with the lyre she is the fat and fiddly one about twenty-four and bossy with red hands and legs nicked from lousy cheap blades still I get my lyre and while I cannot play it I tell them where and how they must precisely lash it to the headboard they are nominally under my orders but there seems to be some deficiency ailing my speech some days leaving me beyond their ken they beyond mine some days I am remarkably improved to the point where I can call my maman's house in Grenoble and find she is away sailing or out shopping or flown off on Concorde or at the parlour being beautified what flusters me most is the overall slide the crumble I'm terribly anxious about wars and such but would like to discuss my funeral arrangements with someone in authority the nurses are hopeless in that regard they watch me through slitted eyes they wait apparently trying to sketch some future I am no longer a part of it is all so petty but why should I bother I can be composed I can be the picture of grace but it's much more fun being gross and fraught

Nora

I don't think he quite appreciates how it is but just because we're at it like a pair of demented bunnies doesn't mean we're a couple.

Novelty Knickers

Shockingly early in the a.m. there's a phone call from someone called Carol Anne at Channel Four and she says her people want me to appear on some late-night show they're putting out. Appears that someone influential has seen the tape of my expletive-laden Old Trafford performance which dear old impossible Nick was supposed to erase. They're offering a four-hundred-quid fee so that pretty much sways me if I wasn't already giddy at the prospect of showing off on television, albeit late-night, albeit Channel Four, which to my mind has rather lost its way since the Dani Behr era. Also four hundred means a flying sortie to Top Shop plus another week's rent covered. From what I know of late-night C4, bare skin seems *de rigueur* so may have to pop in to Claudine at Lelouch's on the Finchley Road for a wax and either a take-home bottle of tan top-up she recommends – never know whether you work that goo right to the tips of your fingers or stop at the wrists – or better yet opt for thirty minutes on the sunbed. Go to meet up with Laura at her office and we walk through Soho Square and go for coffee at this bookshop, Bibliopolis, and sit in the window, streetside, making spectacles of ourselves to all and sundry on the Charing Cross Road. Laura's purse sits open on the high round table between our cappuccinos and shared wedge of poppy cake and the crumbs of our instantly consumed kiwi tartlets, and I can see in the small clear plastic ID fold her favourite photograph showing herself and her exiled boyfriend, Douglas Foggit, the two of them embracing virtually *in flagrante* during an office Christmas party on top of someone's cluttered desk, Foggit's vacuous stare latched on to Laura's sheer-nyloned crotch as exposed beneath her snagged seasonal red tartan skirt; snagged by his hand plus a fortuitously positioned brown and tan Rexel Gazelle paper stapler; in the larger framed print which she keeps at home you can even discern the stapler's British patent number, which presently escapes me, and on that same larger 16×20 print it's further possible to make out beneath her hosiery's stretched weave, the bright reindeer-decorated panties she's wearing; frisky, bright-nosed, bright-pizzled bull reindeers in fact. My belief is that fun panties are best avoided as they're always likely to come back to haunt you. But I don't say anything now, make no enquiry as to Foggit and how the two of them are getting along. It's tough maintaining a relationship with someone who lives three thousand miles away; unless you're in the shipping business and can courier evocative love tokens, Thermos-flasked juices, fresh clippings, and suchlike, at no excessive expense and on the spur of the moment, spontaneity being a boon at all events. Presently we're occupied by other affairs. Mine.

'So, you're not going to see him again?' asks Laura.

'No,' I say, shaking my head, 'he wants me to meet his mother. What's that tell you?'

And she goes, 'He's a normal nice regular human being of the male variety and we all know how awash the world is with specimens of that quality.'

And I go, 'Look, men either want to keep you captive and turn you into their mothers, or else they want to rip out your beating heart as a prelude to dumping you, and neither prospect really appeals. So, what you have to do is get in ahead of them, smite them before they smite you.'

And she goes, 'Smite? Who says smite?'

And I go, 'It's a word.'

And she goes, 'You know that you're nuts.'

And I go, 'I can't do this right now. I have a career to think about. I have a book to write.'

And she goes, 'Which book? The Cantona book or the Beckham book?'

And I go, 'Don't be harsh. You know perfectly well which book. *Rupert Murdoch and the Decline of English Football*.'

And she goes, 'The what?'

And I go, 'I am going to write this book. This book is the most important thing in my life at the moment.'

And she goes, 'Don't walk away from this man. Don't let him get away. I have a feeling this is the right one for you.'

And I go, 'And you would know?'

And she goes, 'Yes, I would, as a matter of fact.'

And I go, 'And I should just settle for one?'

And she sees me for what I am, she knows me, she goes, 'When it feels like you can have them all?'

And I go, changing the subject, 'Could you manage some more cake?'

And she nods her head and I raise my hand, trying to get the girl's attention.

Orla

It was the end of the summer. Bunting hung snagged across telephone wires from some forgotten carnival. She wore a yellow-and-blue blouse, the colour of that bunting. All summer we'd laughed and dived off rocks into the river, aware of the boys who spied on us from the overgrown banks. It was a jungle. Our long hair streaming behind us in the cold water, we slipped and slid and clutched at each other, laughing uncontrollably. So much was expected of us. We were academically bright and physically alert. Everything happened so fast. We were nearly flipped inside out with delight. Nothing was meaningless. The world whirled in a frenzied orbit around us. Her baby cousin laughed and threatened to put her finger up our bottoms if we didn't give in to her. At four she already had rowdy boyfriends who taught her to say such things. We laughed at her and told her to scram. Where there is light there are shadows and if you hang around long enough they get to you. We talked about rewinding the plot and reinventing ourselves but that wasn't possible. We held each other motionless for hours, reluctant to break the embrace, inhaling each other's breath, our limbs falling dead. I tried to guess what would remain after she'd leave. Memories are so imponderable. We made ink drawings on each other's skin. We scrubbed the ink from each other sitting in our bath, staining the ceramic. She had dates lined up for when she got home to the city, though she assured me they were all platonic, long-standing obligations she could not hope to evade. The ink was deep in some of our pores and needed wearing away over time. I wanted us to cut each other to the quick with a diver's knife I'd stolen from my brother-in-law. I wanted us to share the same scars. When I suggested this, she looked at me for ages like I was a stranger to her, and then she sobbed and ran off without saying goodbye. Not long afterwards her parents drove down from the city and took her away. I knew if she returned the following summer she would have changed into someone more confident and precise and she would have forgotten our lust. I wrote to her through the winter in a doomed rearguard action. I knew I would never get away from her. I knew she was gone from me. I knew I would never see her, or if I did, she would not be the same girl. She was made for the real world where love must be practical. For ages I thought about slashing and tearing myself. Life is pyrrhic. She left me nothing but some eyeliner, an old sweater and a selection of gum wrappers. I knew I would never go with a man. I knew I would never know love again. Love appalled me. The anguish was deafening. No one looked for me any more.

Phone Calls

The phone rings, once and no more, as if the caller has had a change of heart or a lapse of nerve. These are always the calls I ache to pick up because I sense they are the ones that would, if only they could reach me, change my life for ever and better, and even, incidentally, spruce up the caller's own dour, thread-bare existence.

Pickup on Hyperion Ave

None of this hardly matters. Does it? Like whether or not I take it in the backway from a man I've just now met though apparently I know his brother from somewhere. Some street corner or other he seems to be suggesting. Some other time. Escapes me. I want to explain how none of that hardly mattered then. Never mind now. Something tells me he's got the impression I like to get it painfully. At least some of the time. Like when I have a choice. I try to explain. Which is a struggle. Without coming across as some great big block of ice. Then again, what do I care.

Pigpoo

. . . like my mother says, you always know where you stand with a pig by your side . . . this may seem unduly cynical when applied as she very much intended to all her dealings with men . . . but she's had more than her share of misfortune where love's concerned . . . and I wouldn't be her daughter if I didn't take heed and apply to my own affairs some of the more difficult lessons she's learned over the years . . . so I rarely get into anything interface-wise with high hopes of a great everlasting romance . . . I keep it simple . . . no clinging . . . no desperate craving for long-term commitment or fidelity . . . no dreaming of elaborate nuptials or honeymooning in the Seychelles . . . no wishful speculative shopping trips to Mothercare or Baby Gap or for that matter Baby Ikea . . . a little bit of pleasure, a modicum of fun, and I'm content, the proverbial happy bunny . . . that's all I need in principle . . . plus of course a tolerance for pigpoo . . . masses and masses of pigpoo.

Rodeo Star

This is what happens seven or eight weeks ago. A heavy-set farmer, reminds me of my father, which of course should tell me something, gets me into bed. It takes him twenty seconds from start to finish. Then he wants to talk. I lock myself in the bathroom. When I come out again he's in the kitchen waiting for me to feed him. I tell him he's got the wrong woman. He leaves. I smoke one cigarette and then another. I go for a drive rather than stay in the house. Driving all night. Wishing I had a gun. I'd cull the ones who aren't cut out for love.

Remembering from somewhere that eight seconds in the saddle makes a rodeo star.

Sex With My Husband

This is another man. Call him Steve. Call him Harry. Call him in from the fields. He's right here with me. Now. In my room. His tongue hanging. His hands twitching. His legs shaking. His pupils dilated. A big chunk of wood directed at me. He's going to plough me. He's got a ring in his brow. A small gold ring shining over his left eye. His skin's the colour of peat, his nails are cracked and his muscles hard from labouring in the sun. He shoves his tongue in my ear as a prelude. His hot tongue. He licks my neck, my throat. He bites my shirt-covered breasts. One bite for each breast. Then he lays me out on the bed, my bare legs dangling, my skirt thrown up to my waist, and he puts it in me. All the way inside of me. His hot prick touches the cold end of my womb. He's ploughing me. Ploughing me. Ploughing me. He won't look me in the eye. And I won't make a sound. I'm like a mouse while he's ploughing me. He thinks he's the beast. He believes. I say nothing. I do nothing. He grunts and groans, doing the ploughing, all the ploughing. They're all of them the same. Smell and touch and weight and means. Just like my husband.

Smoking

When we first moved up here from the country I had
this friend, Victoria, I got to know from school. We did
all the usual friend things girls do growing up. Then one
day we're lying out on the lawn, the sun shining, on this
grassy slope, sharing a stolen cigarette. But this time is
different from all the other times we've been together,
because when I turn my head I can see a big dark nipple
through the V of her shirt, some of the buttons aren't
done all the way up. It's the size and shape of a
raspberry, the colour of a bruise. And she says to me,
'You ever try and picture your parents in the sack?' And
I look at her, thinking if I look as terrified as I'm feeling
then she must really be laughing at me. And she makes a
fist and pushes it back and forth like she's slowly
stabbing something, somebody. And I take the smoke
from her and close my eyes and drag real hard until I
think I'm going to pass out. And when I open my eyes
again I'm totally surprised to find her still lying there
alongside me, still waiting for my answer. And then she
pulls up one knee so her skirt falls back and she
scratches her bare thigh and she's got blue cornflowers
scattered across her bright white panties. 'No,' I say,
'do you?' And she catches me out again, saying, 'You
mean do I picture your parents or mine?' And I say,
'Either.' And she says, 'Both. Is that weird or what?'
And her eyes narrow to slits in this bold clever

precocious way and she reaches out to take the dying cigarette from my fingers and I don't know any more from that moment what kind of world I've fallen into.

Snakeproof

It oughtn't to have been propitious, and it wasn't, but he made out like it was and worked extremely hard at persuading me. The first time I went out with him he vomited in the taxi, vomited on my dress, my shoes, my hair, vomited everywhere. Everyone said he was a wonderful boy and I married him four months later because he made me laugh and he was pretty and his people had money and whole chapters to themselves in the history of the republic and he convinced me I was beautiful and I was already pregnant and thought I understood what it meant to be happy. This went on for a long time, years even, and his devotion to me throughout that time was more than a little gratifying. It would be mischievous not to admit that it crammed me with delight. Now, however, I suspect he always thought me a little shallow and unsuitable. Fine, I could dance and fish and sail and cook and sew and do the garden and make a swell rum punch and a better *poulet au vinaigre* and chitchat with the neighbourhood clergy and the swishest of the boardroom wives and drop his children off at school at Holy Child and Blackrock but there was always something not quite right about me, some dreary subcutaneous component. I have no idea what it was, but it wormed away at his affection for me and in his mind it was the origin of my downfall. I've spent a lot of money in the vain hope of discovering the flaw in me that in the end sent him away. While I was with him I did everything I thought I should do to make him happy. I ironed his socks, his underpants, his shirts. I deferred to him in politics and sports. I swallowed his sour-tasting semen with a smile. I bore him his children. I suffered his illnesses with him. I swum in his wake. I declined to drive his cars or use his cameras, which were apparently beyond any aptitude I might have. I tolerated his patting my behind in some approximation of public affection. And still the secret flaw in me chewed away at him until one day it snapped something inside of him or me and it became base and unbearable. We were sent hurtling into free fall as he ceded me the house in Monkstown and moved south along the coast to an altogether grander Killiney outcrop. He made even that sound considerate as he insisted on remaining close to the children and granting me generous terms. He suggested we retain a footing as friends. I obliged as ever, Mrs Amenable, but there wasn't a word forthcoming as to why I was suddenly so rank. He would call sometimes and berate his own callousness in setting me aside but never once did he abuse me or indicate specifically what it was about living with me that had become so unbearable. Then he openly took up with Elaine Harnedy, an account executive at his company. She is a talkative, blonde, famished creature, half my age, a quarter my size, and her unveiling in public, as it were, went some way to clarifying the issues which most vexed me. I am aware of the risk of growing shrill. I bear up, maintain appearances, dress well. Jerzy in Redz does my hair, Thursdays, at ten. I entertain no illusions that I know of. I cater loyally for old friends and family. I vacation chastely in Tenerife and Barbados. Still, I can't stop thinking I should cut out his gizzard and feed it to his children.

Stephanie's Reeboks

He's on the floor, I'm talking about Jason now, he's on the floor, his back to the wall, reading a magazine, and I'm kneeling by his feet, painting his toenails, and I go, 'Jason,' and he goes, 'Mmm?' and I go, 'Would you ever lie to me?' and he goes, 'Only if my life depended on it,' and I go, 'So you don't mind telling me how many girls you've slept with?' and he goes, 'Girls?' and I go, 'It's a two-parter actually, A, how many girls? and B, how many guys, oh, and maybe a minor supplemental enquiry to deal with the flora and fauna issue,' and he goes, 'Flora and fauna?' and I go, 'Pumpkins, you know, pigs, that sort of thing,' and he goes, 'I don't recall any pigs and definitely no pumpkins,' and I go, 'So, tell me, how many girls?' and he goes, 'I don't know,' and I go, 'Give me a figure,' and he goes, 'I'm sorry, I said I don't know,' and I go, 'Guess,' and he goes, 'I'm sorry,' and I go, 'Was it hundreds?' and he goes, 'God, no,' and I go, 'Dozens?' and he goes, 'I don't remember,' and I go, 'Dozens then?' and he goes, 'No,' and I go, 'No?' and he goes, 'No, not dozens but . . .' and I go, 'But it was quite a few?' and he goes, 'Ah,' and I go, 'OK, so, not such a number as might suggest turpitude but . . .' and he goes, 'What's turpitude?' and I go, 'Dozens,' and he goes, 'It wasn't turpitude,' and I just laugh, and he goes, 'You don't believe me?' and I shake my head, not caring, really, not wanting to cry or anything, and he reaches over and touches me, and I chase him round the room, threatening to disembowel him.

In the end we simply play out this sick fantasy of his. We're in Tuscany, driving through these early-summer green rolling hills, and one of us has to get out and help our son to wee by the side of the road like in that Volvo station wagon from £22,095 newspaper ad. That's him in the car, poring over the map. I get the short straw, holding up Jason Jr., who's dribbling down my shins, weeing right into my new Reeboks. Typical.

Talk

Two hundred pounds an hour for talk. It seemed a joke. Not the money. The notion that talk could be of any use. But the process was still something which I knew I had to explore, even exhaust. My friend Daisy had recommended him in a roundabout way. She'd told me how he'd helped a woman whose daughter had died. I appreciated the care she took not to suggest I needed his help to an equivalent extent. She was merely telling me a story about this other woman. It had nothing to do with me, how I was getting on in my life.

It was raining. Water ran on the big rectangular windowpanes. I was a little wet, having forgotten to bring either a raincoat or an umbrella, and had been compelled to run from my car, a hundred feet or so to the door of his house. I had on a cotton jersey dress, pumpkin-coloured, short-sleeved, collared, with a three-button front, and white tennis shoes, no socks, my hair pinned in a dozen severe tucks. I imagined the man was affronted by my casual style, my glowing face. I imagined he could not be taken in by my bravado. He would not meet my eyes. He would not challenge me. I just started talking. It was like this.

People say I talk too much. Friends. Family. Do you think I talk too much? I probably do. I probably have to confess I like to talk, though I have so little opportunity down here. Enjoy it to the point where it's in danger of becoming something more. Pathological. Morbid. A vice even. This is quite like confession, isn't it, only you don't say very much, do you? Plus, another preconception I had, is, and it's been hit on the head fairly thoroughly, I mean, you're not at all like my mother, which is my recollection of what this was like, from the other time, the only other time I might add. What I thought that this would be again, despite your being the wrong sex of course. I expected you'd mother me with comment and advice and direction, but nothing, not a puff. Is that it? My time's up? Not yet? OK. Will you take a cheque? Or shall we start an account? Unless you think I'm already cured? Is that possible? Am I cured, do you think? Oh, you don't cure? Then, tell me, what do you do? What am I paying you for? What am I about to write you a cheque this instant for? I want to get better. I do. I want to be better. A nicer, more wholesome person, a likeable soul. Attractive even. Lovable. That would be more than I could hope for. And we all seek to be lovable, don't we. I don't understand anything else. Am I being naive? I know I'm not cynical. I believe in love. Are you married? Was she ever your patient? Am I talking too much for you? I need to believe in love. I always have and I always shall. My friend, I don't love him but we see quite a lot of each other. He told me I looked like a Vietnamese tart in this dress. He surprised me. Using such a word. I doubt he's known many tarts in his time let alone Vietnamese ones. I mean, you don't see that many down this way, do you. It may have been my colouring he was commenting on, not that I'm especially dark, you know. Of course it's short, the dress I mean, but it's not, you know, slit up to heaven, but Lord, I like it, and I'm the one has to take it all on the chin. Comments like that. I could change I suppose and not have to suffer them. Dress down. But then I might as well take up wearing sackcloth, a paper bag over my head, give up speaking altogether for fear of offending someone out there I don't hold in any regard whatsoever, doesn't care a whit about me, why should I, what I may have gone through to get this far, why should I worry about them. That's what kills me. A dread I may have lived according to other people's lights and not been entirely true to myself. I realise only now how that would be the greatest tragedy. Tell me if I'm talking too much. Because you have to tell me to shut up if I'm boring you. You absolutely do. I'd hate that. Thinking I'd paid you to sit there, bored out of your wits, taking it on the chin on my account. The money, yes, I know. And you do look like you care. Honestly. I didn't mean to just now, you know, deride that side of your job. But, seeing as I'm paying you, it is a business after all, am I right? May I ask you something? Do you find me attractive? No, of course I don't go around asking people I've just met, are you serious, is that how I come across? Oh, really. No, no, not at all. Hardly, anyhow. I'm sorry, it's just I'm sometimes curious about the impression I make on people. Like with that tart comment. A Venetian, sorry, Vietnamese tart. That, I find difficult to fathom. My boyfriend? Funny, that's about the last word, that's not exactly how I think of him, no. Quite a bit older in fact. Of course, it may have been perfectly innocent. But you wonder. One wonders. In one's quieter moments. Not brood exactly. You know I'm going to be forty-four this September. I don't mind telling *you* that's superficially gotten me in the jaws of some sort of, I don't know precisely, paralysis, yes, that's it. Which I suspect is where you come in. Why I allowed myself to submit to this whole procedure. And please don't mention vanity. Or throw my looks back in my face. That has nothing to do with this. Absolutely. I know you never. Look, I do appreciate that. Frankly, I have to tell you, I don't hold much with your profession, your high profession. But it's my time and my money and I can do whatever I choose. Even something so utterly incredible and, excuse me, *sorcerous* as this. Well, it is. Faintly. And redolent, you agree, of that sort of, well, dark mystique. Is redolent too strong? I don't mean stinking, to demean what you do here, but I have my doubts and reservations, which I'm entitled to. Yes, I'm sceptical. But then again I am here now, talking to you. About to give you my cheque for my money. Until another time, then. Is that how we shall leave it. Christ, I've offended you, haven't I? No, *thank* you.

For this I pay the man two hundred pounds. Am I nuts or am I fruit? You tell me. I doubt he has the answer. Perhaps if I see him again I'll challenge him.

The First Time . . .

The first time I tried to kill myself I went out to Dollymount Strand, ate four chocolate eclairs, two dozen paracetamol, drank the most of a half-pint of Haig Scotch, passed out, came to with a dog licking my face, managed to crawl into the sea, drank salt water until I threw up, and then I went home. Do I try to kill myself often? Couple of times a year. Another time I hanged myself with my tights. Pretty Polly opaques. But the crotch gave and I fell four feet onto my backside. I was black and yellow for weeks after that, top and bottom, couldn't swim, go to PE, wear anything low-cut or without an arse to it. It was so embarrassing going around all wrapped up like a fucking nun. But I don't think anyone really noticed, or missed anything, you know.

The Hon Mary A

After the divorce I devoted years upon years to a growing child and a number of short-lived romances; a number, neither large enough to indicate depravity, nor low enough to suggest a life without frolic. I wouldn't even term them romances, though I consider they were never the opposite, cheap or ugly engagements, tawdry amourettes. There was always in those liaisons, if only initially and for an instant before disappointment invariably flooded in, the illusion, the promise of more, of gentleness and intimacy, affection and regard. In retrospect they all seem part of a sad patchwork of lukewarm strangers . . . well-schooled, well-heeled, determinedly enterprising types, deal-makers, professionals, amateur sportsmen, adventurers, travel writers . . . who neither mistreated nor misled me. They came, at little or no notice from their busy schedules, expecting clean sheets and cheerful good-natured sex on tap. They came, sometimes furtively, oft-times brazenly. The married ones, I noticed, always reserving a thought or two for their absent wives. And increasingly, as the years advanced, these men, either discreetly or blatantly, let their focus drift from me and sought instead news of Joely, whiffs of her presence or passing, glimpses of her either in photos or the flesh. I cannot blame them for that. Though neither can I bear the memories of their time with me, so suggestive are they all of wasteful usage.

The Kiss

One time, my mother said to me, 'Remember there's no one to save you, only yourself, and you'll never be hurt, never be disappointed.'

'What about love?' my father had said, which astonished us both because we hadn't thought he was listening, and besides, he never raised such notions or spoke such words.

He smiled and winked at me and I thought, yes, he'd save me, yes, he would.

And my mother said in mild despair, 'Oh, what are you saying to the girl?'

And he took her in his big rough hands and drew her close, making her smile with expectation, and he kissed her, his unshaven face pressing against her soft skin. He kissed her, a lingering soft kiss, there before my eyes, in the kitchen of this very house. And I knew they'd die, and I as well, and I didn't look away for one moment, kept on looking at them, soaking up the picture of their embrace, the kiss that seemed to last for ever. My mother and father, when they were alive, when they were my age, older, kissing, right here in this house.

The Lido

Another day and sleep restores nothing. We go down in waves at the lido. A buxom lass with thighs kept pale and rich in secret under wraps all winter lustres quickly. We burn so badly no one can touch us. Our mothers will be so relieved. And as our fortnight runs out, our impatience erupts. We need release from our eternal chaste vacation. What is the alternative? There is nothing new, nothing to be discovered only more of the same. The natives are so variegated from a distance but in our fists, up close, the dross is just the same. Uncertainty and menace, these are our suitors. The attendant, Diego, offers a showing of his well-used genitals. He is handsome enough even if his nails are begrimed. He has white, white teeth in a wildly optimistic smile. We are certain he will join us in bed, the price not discussed, that to be brokered after the fact. We've heard how sometimes these people even think you're going to marry them, whisk them away to a life in some dreary damp northern suburb. He has such fine shoulders, a handsome chest, and the well-hung parts we have spent years telling each other we ideally long to encounter. The guide, Pilar, our favourite, announces she is pregnant. Her boyfriend is indignant at the claim. We don't understand the ins and outs of the affair. He threatens to send the lot of us down in flames. He thinks we are talking about him, his precious free-ranging manhood being reined in by a sudden swarm of domestic obligations. On the other hand, Diego kisses each of us and clutches at our bottoms and imparts somehow to each a sense of separate significance. None of us are on the pill. We have diaphragms, coils and rubbers. Mandy favours a Bulgarian spermicide. I favour Diego's swearing on his mother's heart he will leave before he comes. I applaud his syntax. He wants me to point out my clitoris. I ask him what about all the others, had none of them a clitoris. He asks to shine a torch on me. I am flattered momentarily and decline. I am always declining, he tells me. He spits in my hair. I cannot cry, not now. He demands to be left in the bathroom while I sit on the loo and vacate noisily. And then he orders . . . tells me to change into a favourite flattering dress and slaps me about the shoulders quite jovially. I think he likes me almost as much as the virgin at the lido.

The Porn Business

I meet this doctor at this party thrown by some people I scarcely know, at least he tells me he's a doctor, he's so good-looking, tall, young, neat, well-mannered, and he introduces me to his friend who's as attractive and soft-spoken, they could be brothers, and anyway to cut a long story short they're making this documentary about virgins and sex and want me to appear in it, and I'd like to because I like them but I'm not that dim since they're upfront about there being a very minute amount of essential, discreet, tasteful nudity involved and I'm flattered naturally and I find them hilariously amusing and diverting but they're really busy, too busy to wait for me to make my mind up, in an absolute tear to make this film, and I see them going around picking up girls, most of whom strike me as anything but virginal, and anyway they go off somewhere with their video camera and come back a short while later all smiles and joking together like they've shared in some gentle amusing rite of passage and then I don't run into them again and they don't call and I see the girls sometimes and mean to ask them what it was really all about but don't have the courage to go up to them in case it was something sordid like I honestly deep down expected and understood but nevertheless I'm left with a feeling that was a road I'm half-glad half-regretting I've not gone down.

The Price

I'll fuck anyone. You don't have to be good-looking or young or strong or healthy or anything. You don't have to have hair or teeth or nice skin or all your own limbs or even your wits. You could be fat and smelly and warts on you like leaky lemons and hands like proper butcher cudgels and dribbling with famishment and lust and excitement and I don't care. Believe me. You just have to meet my price. You just have to have the right amount of shiny shekels in your hand. That's my code. My morality. Straight as a die. That way it's clear. That way there's no scope for giving or receiving confusion or offence.

Toasterbaby

So I tell her the female equivalent of a nerd is a needy which is someone crying out for a makeover and buckets of affection applied in the most tactile ways imaginable. And I tell her she's not a needy, she's a toasterbaby, waiting to pop. And what does she do? She breaks it all off, won't even talk to me, and I was only paying her a fucking compliment.

Tom Cruise

I would condemn myself for one word, one touch, one kiss. I'm talking about Tom Cruise. He's becoming, I think, like the Cary Grant of our times. I'd certainly permit him anything he wanted. Access all areas.

Toyboy

I remember him flirting with me, the most forthright
and fearless of the shirtless crew, not a pick of spare
flesh on their bones, and the midsummer morning after
they'd finished the job, he returned unannounced,
looking for a spirit level he claimed to have left behind,
and uncharacteristically I helped him look for it, walking
barefoot, bouncy from my morning coffee, still finding
the agreeable taste of it, feeling bright and young, my
loose hanging hair still wet from my shower, confident
in a saffron velour shirt over navy cotton shorts of my
bright appeal, chatting easily to him as I accompanied
him around the looping kerbed perimeter of tarred
black chips, my glazed melon-pink toes sweeping
through the lovely open-faced daisies until I trod on
something coldly metallic, half-buried in the grass, and
holding it aloft, asked him if this was what he was after

Tracking Rory

In the four years since I left him, somehow or other
word of Rory's adventures always seem to find a way
through to me. Irregular but true bulletins, showy
spurs, as if drawn to me by some lasting attraction. He's
been in a road accident and almost died, along with his
then fiancée, Jessica Somebody? Gobert? Rieboujt?

who'd been driving and who'd borne her own share of the impact, a crushed foot and fibula; he'd lost his spleen. He's worked with the actor Eric Cantona on a commercial in Cape Town that was dogged by a rash of street violence, carjackings and unionised extortion. He's been impaled and poisoned by cactus spindles following a fall in Nevada or wherever the Grand Canyon is, and was rushed to hospital, driven by a local PA in his car, a converted hearse, which vehicle as they approached the Vegas hospital was mistaken by a waiting crowd for the one due to remove the remains of the singer Tupac Shakur, who'd just died of gunshot wounds received earlier the same week. He's choked on a chicken bone in a Hong Kong restaurant and been Heimliched in the men's room three times in swift succession by a powerfully built, tattooed, axe-scarred grip from Swindon, attended by five more of his inebriated crew and the six-year-old daughter of the Polish actress he was involved with at the time. Hospitalised overnight as a result of the Heimlich assault – bruised ribs, collateral concern for the contents of his abdominal cavity – as well as the recalcitrant chicken bone, he met and fell for a twenty-nine-year-old intern who looks like someone – 'Beijing-born pop diva and now Hong Kong movie idol, fabulous Faye Wong,' according to my informant. Inside a month he's married Vanessa, Dr Lin, and now they're in Los Angeles, talking to producer Jerry Bruckheimer about doing a movie, and expecting their first child, and I'm terribly happy for him, though I sometimes wonder whether he ever stops what he's doing just to think of me and the years we spent together. He's never once tried to contact me. His love was, after all, finite. His career goes as well as his personal life. And he seems to have cheated death almost as often as I have cheated love.

True Love

Mum tells me how she met my dad and this much is undisputed. She had her eye on this bloke, Gary, drove a blue Manta, couldn't think how to get his attention, no matter how she flaunted herself he never noticed her, so finally she roped in her brother and they went round to where Gary worked and waited until his lunch break and just as he was walking to his car, Uncle Steve, who's barely sixteen at the time, lets on to attack my mum, who of course at this stage is not yet my mum, not yet eighteen, trying to snatch her purse and Gary just sees right through it because he knows who Steve is, doesn't he, he knows whose brother he is, and he's only laughing at the two kids staging a mugging for his benefit, he sits in his car and drives off, chortling and all, I can picture how mortifying it must have been, but my dad, rather my dad-to-be, who's passing by at this same exact moment, sees all what's going on, thinks it's a genuine mugging, stops his car, jumps out, runs over and whacks my Uncle Steve, breaks his nose, sends real hot blood spurting out all over the place, covering all of them, flipping drenching them, and then naturally enough instead of being lauded as the rescuing hero, my dad has to contend with my mum jumping all over him, slapping and punching and yanking his hair and his ears and his woolly pullover, and raining down blows on him, sending him scurrying back to the shelter of his car and then she realises there's maybe something to my dad's behaviour, some valid excuse, some blind unthinking chivalric heroism, and she's mortified again, at her attacking him, at how she's ever going to explain what the whole farrago was all about, she prayed right then and there for the ground to open and take her, but it didn't, the car door opened instead and whatever he said smoothed things and he drove them to the hospital and, waiting while Uncle Steve was getting his busted nose straightened, sitting around, chatting to my mum, led to one thing and another and that's pretty much the start of their ill-starred relationship which you could say peaked and culminated with me.

Valentine

Roses are red, violets are blue. I come on the tide for to show my harpoon. You hope, pretty maiden, to know me quite soon. We'll go out again and will eat vindaloo. Like that summer we spent on our own lonesome two. You puked in my lap and I in your shoe. We ate mostly out of a tin and a bin. You showed me your pants and I wore them for you. You wove me a rope and you saddled me too. You swore we'd be married if I got you some glue. For your heart it was broken by a scrum half with flu. A ruddy rough bugger with fire-eating friends who all swore to love you if you'd give him some kids. Which is why I've come running with roses and glue and a pointy harpoon for to run them all through and to save you from doom with that fever-eyed crew. And pray tell me, sweet, that I'm sure to endure. For I know where you're downy is why I love you.

This is what I have to put up with, this kind of smut, if I ever find out who sent it I'll crucify the bastard and then I'll denounce him as a pervert stalker shitmonger because this sort of bull is destroying my life, you know, my life is not my own with this hanging over me, some wacko out there thinking about me without my consent, you know, writing crap valentines to me, thinking he loves me or something, thinking there's hope for us, a future, well, I'd like to tell him, oh, just fuck, forget it, just, OK, I'm sorry, I can't do this, I have to go now, OK.

Waxed

I'm meeting my new friend Paul for dinner and I'm late
and though I'm telling myself it's not a *date* date, there's
no hiding how excited I am to be seeing him again. Up
to this point we're just friends, though I'm happy to
admit there's a chance we may be in the process of
becoming more than that. I'll always change my plans
for him even if he calls at the very last moment
suggesting dinner or a movie.

Tonight, once I get in the restaurant, I shrug out of
my coat and spot him and wave and I rush to where he's
waiting and we kiss cheeks and I jump right in, telling
him all about my day, how I've just come from my
mother's and how I feel so dull and jaded by comparison
with her vibrant personality, her unflagging social life,
her hectic string of shallow effortless romances. I explain
how she was actually very nice to me. I tell him, though,
how when I was leaving, she asked if I needed anything
and it hit me that a normal mother might mean money or
recipes or a cashmere sweater but with Caroline it was
probably a bikini wax she had in mind or the loan of her
bumper collection of *Better Sex* videos.

And Paul just floors me with what he says next. He
says, 'And would you like a bikini wax?'

And I go, 'Would I what?'

And he goes, 'I do a terrific wax, wax you all the
way up the wazoo, it's all the rage.'

And I don't know what to think. Is he gay? Is he

telling me pain is something he's not averse to meting out? A moment ago I was thinking what a wonderful listener he is. A moment ago I was wondering what it would be like to kiss him, his so very faintly chapped lips which after the first kiss I could legitimately offer to exfoliate for him with the sawn-off toothbrush I've begun to carry in my purse for that very purpose. Now my head hurts and I just can't tell who he is, the man I'm about to have dinner with, the man who's just offered to wax me up the wazoo.

I smile bravely and say, 'Another time, maybe.'

And he says, 'Okey-dokey,' and does a cursory scan of his menu and sets it aside smugly, like he's worked everything out ahead of schedule, which is really no biggie, achievement-wise, seeing as how he's been sat here waiting twenty minutes minimum for me to show, and he starts looking around the room to see who else he knows here, and I find I've lost my appetite and I realise that my mother would intuitively know what to make of the situation, how best to deal with it, and I hate her for that and I hate myself for not being more like her.

When I Was Young . . .

When I was young . . . I'm talking six, seven, eight, nine, ten . . . and my mother used to bring home her dates to meet me, we'd slip into the hallway or the

kitchen and have a hurried whispered conference . . .
giggly or deadly earnest . . . regarding the sweating
stiffening prop waiting nervously in the other room.
Apart from the two of us combined presenting such a
formidably intimidating force only the very brave or the
very thick would bother to linger and persist, there was
always the factor of these men's own impossible frailties
and peccadilloes. Either we scared them away from the
off or else we ran them out of the house without an
explanation or excuse. Over time we both came to
realise that no one was ever going to be good enough
for us. The fun was in watching the poor saps lining up
to take their chances against our impossibly high
standards.

Of course, this outlook didn't last. It couldn't.
Something had to give. And it wasn't me. My mother
was the first and last to crack. One day she just threw in
the towel, brought home the footballer, moved him
right in, making all these unmotherly cooing noises,
going Barbie-Cartland-pink-and-feathery fashion-wise,
making sounds and moves I understood involved foggy
ill-considered notions of a little brother or sister for
poor old solitary me.

Poor old solitary me was never the deciding element
in that initial all-out rut that fuelled them to a trip up
the aisle, after which it was all downhill and blood-
letting recrimination.

Why Are My Thighs . . .

My thighs are so colossal. They cry out for remedial action . . . promptly. It makes no difference to me that Britney Spears is an unfeasible bioentity or that Tori Spelling's drag-down, off-centre implants are a warning to all girls to think twice and all guys to stand clear . . . I still want to be improved and enhanced. Other pressing issues. Must find tickets for *The Vagina Monologues* and share in the confirmation-celebration. What is all the fuss about? Mine never shuts up. Cut all dead meat from diet. Ditto bed. The phenom of bleeding eyeliner needs to be addressed, esp re potential for product which counters same, surely exceedingly lucrative. Mad Margate artist, Tracey Emin, is my jaw-jutting sister in the mirror. If she could talk back I'd ask her how I should go about getting a life. Mere speculation: she'd say, 'You're prettier than me, younger, thinner, fight it, scowl more, downplay your neediness, insist on topside, self-serve in all events, care for your teeth, tweezer whatever suits you, don't smoke, move direct, turbo-charge, don't amble, life stutters and death yawns, mow them fuckwits down.' Also, alas, am flatter-chested. Ballerina's A cups. Therefore more obscure. The bane of my life. No tits. And I can't shake it. Nothing to shake. Nothing. Not a bump, not a zit . . . I hate myself for hating myself for such a shallow reason. Reasons. Am shallow and destined to remain so. Is that so terrible? Jeremy Paxman would know the answer to that. Shall ambush him, peel down my dresstop and have him ponder. Right. In a million years, Paxman.

Wooing

Heather Mary tells this to me, her cousin and close confidante, Heather Belle, in Starcky loo of over-priced hotel restaurant not a gazillion gobs from The Ivy:

Heather Mary was sat at her desk, sipping a Diet liquid through a bendy straw from a take-away plastic container while studying (dispassionately) the cosmetic surgery ads in the back of *Tatler*. Aaron (her boss's ne'er-do-well younger brother which complicates everything) walked up. She flipped the magazine onto its face, rested her elbows on it. They smiled thinly at one another.

'What are you reading?' he asked.

'*Cosmo*,' she answered.

Without so much as a by-your-leave he pulled the magazine from under her elbows, flipped it over, scanned it, looked at her as if she were tragically transparent. She averted her eyes, noisily sucked the last drops of liquid from the container.

He checked her out as he read, 'Furs at wholesale prices? International clairvoyant and celebrity psychic?

Run your own catering business from home? Laser treat unwanted hair, tattoos and other blemishes? Nose reshaping? Ear correction? Breast enlargement? Reduction? All cosmetic procedures at reasonable rates? Parties organised? Fun for all ages?'

'I see right through you,' she declared.

'You do?'

'You're somewhere between a screaming misfit and a flirting arsehole.'

He showed his teeth, said, 'What's that supposed to mean?'

'Keep it up and see where it gets you,' she said, and she snatched the magazine from him and walked off.

'I'm just trying to be friendly,' he called.

She raised a finger in parting shot. And Aaron went, under his breath, though she could still hear him, 'Lesbian.'

And she went back at him in much the same tone of voice, 'Shitheel.'

'You know what this means, don't you?' I say.

'No,' says Heather Mary. 'Tell me.'

I tell her if she wants to sleep with him that's her business and may not be such a retrograde move careerwise. She's appalled and insulted by my forthrightness, my low estimation of her sexual mores and standards re her selection of partners. I shrug and tell her why deny it. She falls into this deep trance state as if she's confronting some inner demon she'd had no inkling existed anywhere in the wide wide world never mind has now glaringly taken up resolute rooty residence within her shiny pinky portals. It's primal, I tell her, we're compelled to fuck the ones we can't abide.

Zest

In the meantime what else is there to do with my body in its prime only engage in more hasty, unconsidered sex, and somehow, in snatches, manage to cover some unclarified issues.

'Do you love me?'

'Oh yeah.'

'Truly?'

'You bet, oh yeah.'

'Like for ever?'

'Oh, baby.'

'No matter what?'

'Absolutely.'

'Because I trust you.'

'That's it, that's good, trust, trust is good, oh . . .'

So intense and passionate is our lovemaking that we fall off the bed, roll and scramble under it, emerge on the other side. He stops up, checks out something he's found, and the mood's transformed. It's the new Ice Age or maybe just the old one all over again.

'What's this?' he says.

'You don't know what that is? I'll give you a clue. You're wearing one. Aren't you?'

'Not one of these, never one of these, never one like this with the ribbing and the, I don't need extra features, do I? No, no, see, see, because I already come equipped with all the extra features any normal woman would be happy to settle for but not you, not the one greatest grotesque mistake I made in my entire life, the one I asked to marry me.'

'Will you forget it.'

'You've been . . .'

'I don't understand you, you're insanely jealous now because you come across an old johnny could be there a dozen years, you're deranged.'

'I'm deranged?'

'You know I don't housekeep. I'm not my mother. I hope you're not turning into a silly chauvinist.' I snatch the offending item away from him and pull it to pieces; nervously destroying the evidence. 'Must be there from before I moved in here. Look, it's all hard and dry and perished.'

'And I'm deranged?'

'Yes, you're deranged. Of course you're deranged. You're the derangest person I've ever known.'

'What about you, Ms Double-Standards?'

'What do you want from me? You know I've been with other men.'

'Since I've met you? Since I asked you to marry me? And I'm deranged? I'm deranged?'

'You're such a baby.'

'You know what you just did? You just broke my heart.'

'You'll get over it.'

'Never,' he says. 'My heart is broken.'

'Please,' I say, wearily. 'I'm with you now, what more do you want?'

'The same as you want from me. The same high standards of, of loyalty, and trust, and exclusivity, and, and . . . not the dizzy urges of a can't-make-up-her-mind trollop.'

I lunge to my feet, throw a punch at him which misses, and fall off balance, hitting my head against the side of the bed. He hurries to check on me. I simply sit up, holding a hand to my face.

'I'm disfigured,' I say. 'I know I'm disfigured. Now . . . I hope your lousy heart is mended.'

He tries to pull my hand away for a look.

'Let me see,' he says.

'Go away,' I say. And tearfully, 'You think I'm a trollop.'

'You're not a trollop.'

Fiercely, 'You called me a trollop.'

'I said . . . what did I say? I'm not sure of my exact words or the context but I'd never call you a trollop.'

'There. You did it again.'

'Beautiful,' he pleads.

'Please, just go,' I say, shaking my head.

I close my eyes for just a moment and when I open them again he's gone. Which is a neat disappearing trick. Now if only I could rid myself of all my other bothers as easily. I go in the bathroom and look in the mirror, finger my face, seeking a bruise. I tend to my essentially unmarked face with a cotton bud and some natural hints concealer goo. A look of preternatural astuteness burning in my eyes. He's coming back. Yes, he is. They always come back for more. This is my mantra, my zesty mantra *du jour*.

Thomas Pynchon

GRAVITY'S RAINBOW

'A supreme teller of tales from the dark underground
of the imagination'
Guardian

'This stunner is already classed with *Moby Dick* and
Ulysses. Set in Europe at the end of WWII, with the V2 as the
White Whale, the novel's central characters race each other
through a treasure hunt of false clues, disguises, distrac-
tions, horrific plots and comic counterplots to arrive at the
formula which will launch the Super Rocket...Impossible
here to convey the vastness of Pynchon's range, the brilliance of his imagery, the virtuosity of his style and his
supreme ability to incorporate the cultural miasma of
modern life.'
Vogue

'Pynchon leaves the rest of the American literary establishment at the starting gate...the range over which he moves is
extraordinary, not simply in terms of ideas explored but also
in the range of emotions he takes you through'
Time Out

VINTAGE

J. G. Ballard

CONCRETE ISLAND

'Ballard's violent exact prose carries you along irresistibly. You believe him, you accept his vision, and it is a fearful one'
Sunday Telegraph

Robert Maitland, a 35-year-old architect, is driving home from his central London office when his car has a blowout and crashes into a traffic island lying below three converging motorways. Maitland climbs up the embankment to flag down a car – but he soon finds that no one will stop, and he is trapped on the island, unable to summon help.

'Ballard writes with taut and precise economy, and the moral of his brilliantly original fable is plain: the interstices of our concrete jungle are filled with neglected people, and one day those people could be ourselves'
Sunday Times

'The challenge of one man thrown onto his own resources is always dramatic, and Ballard explores it brilliantly. Compelling and profound'
Daily Telegraph

VINTAGE

Tibor Fischer

THE COLLECTOR
COLLECTOR

'A work of rare enchantment which could charm a smile out
of a stone'
Daily Telegraph

'So good I promise you will want to read it more than once'
Victoria Glendinning

'Deft, daft and devilishly entertaining, Tibor Fischer's third
novel is narrated by an ancient piece of pottery that appears
to know the secrets of the human heart...The texture of
his prose makes for a deliciously slow read; one savours
the flicker of allusion, the salty humour, the tug of the
sardonic...As slender and exhausting as a supermodel'
Literary Review

'Confirms Fischer as one of the most innovative talents of his
generation...He writes as cleverly as anyone, but he has not
made cleverness his master. His offbeat view of London life
is by turns hilarious and poignant'
Sunday Telegraph

VINTAGE

James Fleming

THE TEMPLE OF OPTIMISM

'A first novel of quite exhilarating brilliance, as richly absorbing a debut as I have read in years. In this marvellous novel one detects the hand of a master. Heart-stoppingly good'
Sunday Telegraph

Anthony Apreece covets the land of his young neighbour, Edward Horne. Edward covets Daisy, Anthony's wife. In this tale of greed and love, James Fleming has recreated 1788 country life in all its extraordinary richness, and a remarkable story that bears comparison with the great novels of the nineteenth century.

'A beautifully written, highly accomplished first novel, his vigorous and poetic prose, flawless dialogue, rich and comical cast of characters and his exquisite observations of period detail make this a feast of a novel'
Mail on Sunday

'Magnificent...Extremely funny and superbly written'
Harpers & Queen

VINTAGE

A SELECTED LIST OF CONTEMPORARY FICTION
ALSO AVAILABLE IN VINTAGE

☐ GRAVITY'S RAINBOW	Thomas Pynchon	£7.99
☐ CONCRETE ISLAND	J. G. Ballard	£6.99
☐ THE COLLECTOR COLLECTOR	Tibor Fischer	£6.99
☐ THE TEMPLE OF OPTIMISM	James Fleming	£6.99
☐ NEWTON'S SWING	Chris Paling	£6.99
☐ HOPEFUL MONSTERS	Nicholas Mosley	£7.99
☐ THE WHITE BOY SHUFFLE	Paul Beatty	£6.99
☐ DESTINY	Tim Parks	£6.99
☐ THE ORCHARD ON FIRE	Shena Mackay	£6.99

- All Vintage books are available through mail order or from your local bookshop.
- Payment may be made using Access, Visa, Mastercard, Diners Club, Switch and Amex, or cheque, eurocheque and postal order (sterling only).

☐☐☐☐☐☐☐☐☐☐☐☐☐☐☐☐

Expiry Date:_____ Signature:_____

Please allow £2.50 for post and packing for the first book and £1.00 per book thereafter.

ALL ORDERS TO:
Vintage Books, Books by Post, TBS Limited, The Book Service,
Colchester Road, Frating Green, Colchester, Essex, CO7 7DW, UK.
Telephone: (01206) 256 000
Fax: (01206) 255 914

NAME:_____

ADDRESS:_____

_____

_____

Please allow 28 days for delivery. Please tick box if you do not
wish to receive any additional information   ☐
Prices and availability subject to change without notice.